I thought I'd never see you again.

But all I have to do is sing our song, and you'll be there...

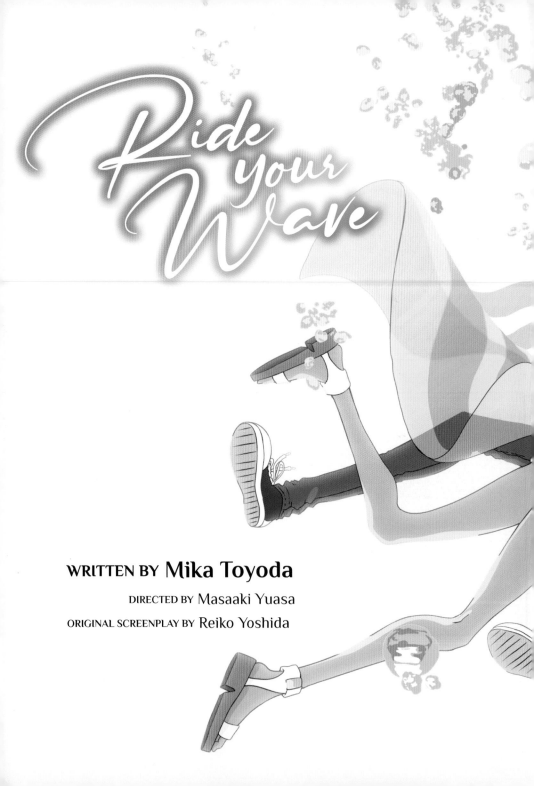

Ride your Wave

WRITTEN BY **Mika Toyoda**

DIRECTED BY Masaaki Yuasa

ORIGINAL SCREENPLAY BY Reiko Yoshida

CHARACTERS

Mukaimizu Hinako

A college student who loves to surf but otherwise has no idea where she's going in life. When a fire breaks out at her apartment complex, Minato comes to her rescue, and she falls in love with him.

ORIGINAL CHARACTER DESIGN SHEETS

Hinageshi Minato

A competent firefighter with a strong sense of duty. When he was young, a little girl saved him from drowning...and to this day, he watches her surf from the station rooftop.

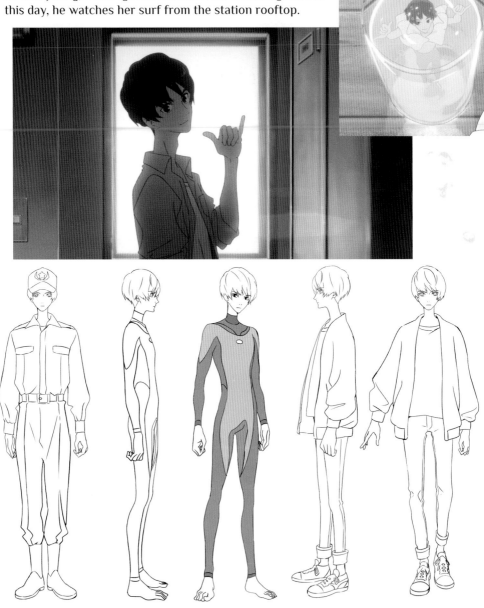

Hinageshi Youko

Minato's teenage sister. She has a snippy attitude with just about everyone, but she loves her brother very much.

Kawamura Wasabi

A rookie firefighter with less experience than Minato. He's a friendly guy, but at work, he's a mess.

SCENE 1

The iconic underwater kiss scene—right as they touch,
Minato turns into bubbles and vanishes. Each character was
drawn separately and then positioned together onscreen.

SCENE 2

Minato is supposed to be dead, yet Hinako keeps seeing him in water. Skeptical, she leaps out into the river. Hinako's motions and the water's splash were drawn separately.

SCENE 3

Hinako and Youko are trapped in a burning building. As
water pours from the top floor, they surf their way down in
one marathon stretch, all while stars twinkle behind them.
The nightscape and waves were drawn separately.

SCENE 4

Hinako and Minato take the next step in their relationship, deepening their bond with a kiss on the pier as the sunset sparkles behind them. The background key frame was drawn separately from the characters, featuring detailed notes.

Ride your Wave

SHOSETSU KIMI TO, NAMI NI NORETARA
by Mika TOYODA
screenplay by Reiko YOSHIDA
concept by Masaaki YUASA
© 2019 Mika TOYODA
© Ride Your Wave Film Partners
© KC
All rights reserved.
Original Japanese edition published by SHOGAKUKAN.
English translation rights in the United States of America, Canada and the United
Kingdom arranged with SHOGAKUKAN through Tuttle-Mori Agency, Inc.

Seven Seas press and purchase enquiries can be sent to
Marketing Manager Lianne Sentar at press@gomanga.com.
Information regarding the distribution and purchase of
digital editions is available from Digital Manager CK Russell
at digital@gomanga.com.

Seven Seas and the Seven Seas logo are trademarks of
Seven Seas Entertainment. All rights reserved.

Follow Seven Seas Entertainment online at
sevenseasentertainment.com.

TRANSLATION: Molly Lee
COVER DESIGN: KC Fabellon
INTERIOR LAYOUT & DESIGN: Clay Gardner
PROOFREADER: Jade Gardner, Brian Kearney
LIGHT NOVEL EDITOR: E.M. Candon
PREPRESS TECHNICIAN: Rhiannon Rasmussen-Silverstein
PRODUCTION MANAGER: Lissa Pattillo
MANAGING EDITOR: Julie Davis
ASSOCIATE PUBLISHER: Adam Arnold
PUBLISHER: Jason DeAngelis

ISBN: 978-1-64827-120-5
Printed in Canada
First Printing: February 2021
10 9 8 7 6 5 4 3 2 1

Ride your Wave

NOVEL BY
Mika Toyoda

TRANSLATION BY
Molly Lee

Airship

Seven Seas Entertainment

Table of Contents

Prologue

"JUST LIKE OLD TIMES!"

These were the first words that left Hinako's lips as she stood on the balcony of her brand-new apartment up on the eighth floor. It was a bright and sunny spring afternoon—and nothing but ocean for miles around. Not some peaceful, idyllic ocean either. The waves around Chiba Sotobo had a mind of their own.

The ocean breeze blew against her head-on, and as the waves swelled, her body itched restlessly. *I mean, just look at that one! Agh!*

"Those hollow waves...!"

The lip of the waves descended steeply as they broke.

Hinako loved, loved, *loved* the ocean—so much so, she'd gone out of her way to apply to the seaside college back in her hometown. So what was she waiting for?!

She pulled her surfboard away from the railing, tucked it under her arm, and slipped between the piles of cardboard boxes to the front door.

Some people spent their formative childhood years in the mountains, while others spent theirs on the beach. Hinako felt that those experiences went on to have a profound impact on everything that came afterward. Depending on your familiarity with the water, your whole life could be completely different!

In Hinako's case, she had spent the first six or seven years of her life right on Kujukuri Beach in Chiba Prefecture—where she was now headed—so the water was practically her second home.

You can take the girl out of the ocean, but you can't take the ocean out of the girl.

Every day she longed for nothing more than to be in the water; whenever she wasn't able to visit the beach, she was so devastated, she barely ate. Was her obsession kind of intense? Yeah. But that was just the kind of girl she was.

As her mother always said, Hinako was so comfortable with water that she overstayed her welcome in the womb by a full ten days. Only after the amniotic fluid was gone had baby Hinako finally been willing to leave.

The porpoise decal on the front of her bright orange surfboard grinned up at her as she loaded it onto the cargo rack of her dark orange bicycle. Then Hinako hopped on and breezily set off for the beach. As she pedaled, the smell of the sea deepened, and the sound of the waves grew closer. Then she entered a tunnel under the elevated toll road—affectionately referred to as "Surf Street" by the locals.

In just a few seconds, she would be mere steps away from the Pacific Ocean. *Eeee, so exciting!* What could possibly be more thrilling than this very moment?

And so Hinako sailed out into the bright sunshine waiting for her on the other side.

"So, whatcha making for dinner tonight?" asked Kawamura Wasabi, a twenty-year-old junior firefighter, as he folded the newly dried sheets.

As it happened, tonight's staff meal was fried chicken. But Minato didn't answer. Instead, he climbed the metal ladder to the highest point on the top-floor terrace: the roof.

All across the world, there were plenty of pretty oceans—the deep blue of the Mediterranean Sea, or the Great Barrier Reef (so large as to be visible from space!), or the clear waters hailed as a "diver's paradise" in the Southern Hemisphere. But to Minato, Kujukuri's chunk of the Pacific was a cut above the rest.

He couldn't actually remember his early childhood (a natural phenomenon known as "childhood amnesia," supposedly) but as far as he knew, he had been born listening to those waves, feeling that sea breeze against his skin, and gazing out at the horizon over that water. Even now that he was a full-fledged firefighter at age twenty-two, he couldn't imagine ever growing tired of it. The best part of his job? This view, right here.

It was early April. The weather was unusually warm, and the ocean's sparkle was exceptional. It was the season of short sleeves, and the firefighters were all wearing T-shirts bearing the symbol of the fire department: a snowflake, intended to represent *water, unity, and purity.*

Minato stood at the far corner of the roof and folded his arms. The crisp ocean air tickled his elbows.

I can't believe it.

Amid the glitter of the afternoon sun on the water's surface, a lone figure slid over the waves.

"Senpai?" Wasabi followed him up the ladder and walked up next to him.

"She came back," Minato muttered to himself.

Dubiously, Wasabi looked out at the ocean. At some point the wind had shifted direction, and now the waves were headed offshore. He could make out a single surfer in the distance; her board was bright orange, and...was that a dolphin decal? She was wearing a yellow bikini, with her hair tied up in a big bun. He couldn't make out the features of her face, but he could tell she was of slight build. She was also quite adept at her craft; she did a cutback, then followed up with a killer roller coaster.

"You know her?" Wasabi asked, blinking in surprise as he looked at Minato. Sure, Minato was a good-looking guy who could probably have his pick of the ladies, but he never seemed all that interested in women.

"She's my hero," Minato explained...and with that, he started humming cheerfully.

CHAPTER 1
Paddling

Hinako was by no means the bragging type, but she considered herself pretty good at cooking. Well, compared to cleaning, anyway. She stood at the stove with her smartphone on the counter, checking the recipe as she went. On the menu: fluffy, oozy omurice. As far as dishes went, it was pretty straightforward. Make some chicken rice pilaf, put an omelet on top, and bam. Omurice.

Rice pilaf was the easy part; Hinako had experience making it in home ec class back in high school. It sat ready and plated, quietly awaiting its pale yellow crown. Now for the omelet.

Hinako poured her beaten eggs into the frying pan, which was hot and primed with vegetable oil. Then, rocking it back and forth, she used her long cooking chopsticks to aggressively stir.

So far, so good. The next step was to slide the egg to one side of the pan right before it had time to fully set.

Wait, really? Already? Crap, it's sticking to the bottom! She hastily swapped out her chopsticks for a spatula.

"Rrgh! Nngh!"

Last step: hold the frying pan with one hand and clap your wrist with the other to create a gentle tossing effect. This was apparently more complicated than it sounded, because bits of loose egg went flying everywhere. Making an omelet should have been simple, and yet somehow it was so complex.

Once Hinako had finagled her egg into a less-than-perfect oval shape, it was time to set it on top of the pilaf. For a moment it stayed in place, but then it rolled off to the side, and when she tried to lift it up with her chopsticks, it split apart irreparably.

"Ugh! God!"

Hinako slumped her shoulders and sighed. This wasn't "fluffy and oozy"—it was just scrambled. But, oh well. It wasn't bad for a first attempt...or so she decided to tell herself, anyway. She grabbed her plate and egg-splattered phone and carried them over to the folding coffee table.

She'd spent all yesterday surfing, so her apartment was still little more than two giant, towering piles of cardboard boxes. And it was there, in the valley between them, that she had set up her makeshift dining area. Why did this feel so familiar? Oh, right—it reminded her of the famous Snow Walls of the Tateyama Kurobe Alpine Route.

But this lighthearted comparison was perhaps a mistake, because right as Hinako set her food down, one of those "walls" started to collapse.

"Whoa!"

Hastily, Hinako pushed it back into place. *Whew, that was close.*

Then the stack next to it started to tilt instead.

"Wha?!"

Reflexively, she threw out her right hand to catch it, but then a stack on the left-hand pile started to fall. And when she reached out to support *that* one, the first stack started to tilt all over again.

What the... Give me a break!

And it was that moment, right when Hinako's hands were both occupied, that her cell phone started to ring.

Uh, guys?! Can you stop ganging up on me for a hot minute?!

The screen displayed the identity of the caller: Hinako's mother.

Not your best timing, Mom!

Willing the boxes to behave themselves, Hinako hastily pulled one hand away, snatched up her phone, and then pressed her hand back in place. All was well, until—"Ack!"—the other pile of boxes started to collapse. And if she hadn't slammed her phone hand against them just in the nick of time, they would have turned her into a Hinako sandwich. As it turned out, all those years of surfing had honed her reflexes in surprising ways.

Moving her thumb, Hinako managed to answer the call and switch it to speakerphone. "Uh, hello? Mom?"

"Hi, sweetie. Did you finish unpacking all your boxes?" her mother asked casually, unaware of the war her daughter was presently waging with said boxes.

"Oh, uh...yeah, totally!"

Thank goodness this isn't a video call!

"Have you been getting enough to eat?"

"Yup! Made omurice!"

Gah! The box at the top of the right-hand stack was threatening to fall, and when Hinako pushed it back, one of the lower boxes popped out. Using her hips, she forced it back in.

Meanwhile, her mother laughed. "You and your brother are so alike! He just asked me to make some."

Her mother's omurice was, of course, exquisitely fluffy and oozy. Hinako could picture its perfect oval shape, placed *just so* atop the rice pilaf... One slice of the knife, and it would split neatly in two, releasing its eggy fragrance... Then her brother would take a bite and smile... Times like these, Hinako envied that he had stayed to help out with the family landscaping business.

"How's college?"

"Hasn't—started—yet!"

Gritting her teeth, Hinako firmly stood her ground between the two mountains of boxes. It felt like she was going to split in half.

"I still don't understand why you chose *oceanography* of all things..."

Not this again! Hinako mentally groaned. "I just really! Love! The ocean!"

And there was no ocean where her parents lived—oh crap, the boxes were going to cave in!

"Are you sure you'll be able to handle the coursework?"

I understand you're worried, but now's really not the time! Hinako thought. "I'll be fine, Mom! Gotta go! I'll call you back later!"

Abort mission! Hinako whipped her hands away. Plan B: grab the table and run. But right as she bent down, an avalanche of boxes toppled onto her back. And her skull.

"Ow!"

Then her water glass toppled over, sending its contents spilling across the floor.

"Man, I need to get it together..."

Under Hinako's torso, her shoddy omelet had turned into an egg pancake.

The clear sky reflected off the puddles from last night's rain.

The fire department maintained a daily training regimen. Today's schedule: on-site water hose drills. These particular drills were critical to ensuring swift and precise firefighting.

"Deploy hoseline two!"

"Yes, sir!"

At the squad captain's command, Wasabi ran back to the fire truck. He was decked out in full firefighting gear, including steel-toed boots and a helmet lined with flame-retardant gossamer fabric. Add on an air tank, and it was easily forty pounds' worth of equipment.

Wasabi grabbed the hose from the rack with both hands and ran back. The hose itself was sixty feet long and weighed about twenty pounds. Combined with his loadout, he was now carrying the equivalent of a nine-year-old child.

Wasabi extended the hose in a straight line, ensured the metal fixtures were connected, and then took hold of the nozzle and got into position.

"Deploy the water!"

On Wasabi's signal, the valve was opened, and water rushed down the hose in a powerful torrent that nearly swept him off his feet.

Hanging from the rails of the training building were several flags with flames drawn on them. Wasabi did his best to aim at the flags, but the weight and recoil of the water made it difficult to keep the hose steady.

"Put your back into it, Kawamura!"

"Yes, sir!"

Essentially, it was target practice—no real fire involved.

"Mist! Stream! Max pressure! Mist! Stream!" The squad captain continued to bark orders one after another, carefully dictating the spread and flow of the water, and there was no time to relax.

"Whoa!" As Wasabi fiddled with the nozzle controls, the hose slipped out of his hand and slammed into his face. He fell backwards onto the ground.

"C'mon, Kawamura! What are you doing?! Grab it!"

Wasabi could understand his boss's frustration, of course, but there was no grabbing this thing, not when it was flailing around in midair like a water-spouting dragon. He sat there on the ground, staring blankly up at it as water sprayed everywhere.

"Shut it off!"

Moments later, the hose fell lifelessly to the ground, the last few drops trickling from the nozzle.

"Kawamura!"

Wasabi could hear the squawking of his squad captain, soaked and furious...but he wasn't the only one. A passing bicyclist had been caught in the dragon's rain shower, and she was dripping from head to toe. Wasabi dashed over to her.

"Hey, are you okay?!"

The young woman wore her hair in a bun, with a few stray strands on either side of her head. She shook the water from her face. Her long-sleeved shirt and denim shorts were now completely soaked through.

Ack! She looks like a bedraggled cat! And it's all my fault! Wasabi bowed his head, fully prepared for the woman to scream at him about her ruined makeup or something to that effect. "I'm so sorry, miss!"

"Oh, it's no problem. I've got a swimsuit on under this!" Contrary to his expectations, the woman shrugged and smiled.

That was when Wasabi noticed the orange surfboard attached to her bike rack, and upon further inspection, he realized her tanned features were free of any makeup. She was by no means model-gorgeous, but she had a sweet and charming smile.

Behind him, Wasabi heard the others packing up the training gear.

Suddenly, he realized: this was the same surfer girl Minato had watched from the roof the other day. The decal on her board tipped him off. At the time, he had thought it was a dolphin, but now he could see it was a porpoise.

The woman pulled a towel from her bag and offered it to him. "Here, take this. It's clean, I promise."

"Oh, no, that's not necessary!"

But despite Wasabi's attempt to decline politely, she cheerfully insisted.

"Thank you..." *How could I possibly say no to a smile like that?*

"Consider it yours. My family hands them out every year at New Year's, so I've got a bunch."

Printed on the towel were the words: CONNECTING PEOPLE AND PLANTS — MUKAIMIZU LANDSCAPING, INC.

"Actually, while I have you..." she said, "I'm kinda lost."

"Where are you trying to go?"

"Oh, I'm just trying to get home."

"Okay...?" Wasabi wasn't sure what to say to that. Surely she was old enough to know how to get to her own house.

"See, I just moved here the other day."

Ohhhh, okay. "Do you know the address?"

"Uhhh...I could give you the name of the complex! It's Sunrise Katamiya."

"Oh, the one right next to the construction site?"

"Bingo!" she exclaimed, pointing back at him. "Oh my God, how did you know? That's crazy!"

Bashfully, Wasabi scratched his head. After all, it wasn't every day he got attention from a pretty girl. He could hear the hoses being disconnected from the fire truck; the other firefighters folded them in half, then rolled them up tightly, starting from the crease. This was a surprisingly tricky task.

"Kawamura! Go show her the way!"

Wasabi glanced over his shoulder to find his squad captain smirking at him. *Rrgh! Don't tease me, man!*

"Don't get me wrong, I'd love to, but...I'm still on the clock," he replied, like a total uptight loser. But he was still a rookie, so he was in no position to ditch work early.

"Oh, that's okay! If you could just give me directions, that'd be great."

"No problem. First, take this road all the way to the bright white apartment building, then make a right. From there, take the second left and keep going until you pass by the school. Then make a right, and you should see it."

"Right, left, school, right," she repeated, pointing with her index finger.

"Kawamura! Bring in your damn hose!"

"Yes, sir!" *Crap, I gotta get back to work!*

"All right, see ya!" With a short wave, the surfer girl rode off into the distance.

"Safe travels!" Wasabi called after her. "Try not to get lost again, Miss Hero!"

If only you'd been scheduled to work today, Senpai. Chuckling to himself, Wasabi went back to work.

Hinako raced through the puddles on her bicycle, humming to herself. For some reason, she always felt her best on the day after a good, hard rain. The sky was clear and blue, and the air smelled clean, with no trace of dust. When she was little, she had jumped into rain puddles on purpose, and her mother had always scolded her for it. But now she was grown, and there were no little yellow rain boots to be seen—just a couple of bike tires, leaving ripples in blue and white reflections.

"Right! Left!" Hinako shouted, pointing each way she declared as she followed the directions given to her by that cute firefighter from earlier. "School!"

I did it! I'm here!...Now that I think about it, didn't he call me "Miss Hero" just now? What was that all about?

"Wait, what?" After pedaling for a long while, Hinako came to a slow stop. She looked to the left, looked to the right, looked straight ahead...and frowned. "Where am I, exactly...?"

She was in a residential district she didn't recognize—because she'd forgotten the final instruction to make a right after passing the school.

Just then, Hinako noticed a big truck headed her way, spraying water from the puddles on the road.

"Huh?"

The pedestrians ahead of her were able to quickly turn the corner onto a side street to avoid it, but Hinako was sandwiched between the road and a concrete block fence. There was nowhere for her to run.

"Wait, what? Hold on a minute!" As Hinako floundered helplessly, the truck shot past, spraying her with a giant torrent of gutter water. "Uggghhhh! Why?!"

Now she was soaked all over again. If it had been ocean water or spring water, she wouldn't have minded, but *gutter water*? No thank you! Worse, she'd given her only towel to that firefighter. Desperately, she prayed for the rain to come back and rinse her off. Ideally her face at the very least.

And so, ignoring the weird looks she received from the passersby, Hinako finally arrived back at her apartment. With a big sigh, she closed the door behind her and slumped her shoulders.

First she was crushed under a pile of boxes, then she got lost, then she got sprayed with a fire hose, and then she got splashed with dirty rainwater. What a disaster of a day.

But unbeknownst to her, the biggest disaster was yet to come.

Late that night, Minato was on duty at the fire station, making an entry in the logbook, when the speaker on the office wall started blaring.

"Outbreak in Katamiya district, block 43. Fire has spread to a neighboring apartment complex."

It was a report from the fire department dispatch center, passed on to them from the 119 operator. Two command documents came through the fax machine, complete with status updates and a detailed map. Apparently the fire had originated in the construction site next door to the apartment complex.

Koba, the driver engineer, promptly set about outlining their route and optimal hydrant locations.

"Protective gear, check! Boots, check!"

Meanwhile, as Minato was getting dressed at the lockers, Wasabi came barreling out of the bunk room. "That complex is where your hero lives!"

"What?!"

But there was no time to stand around and panic.

"Pants, check!"

"Lapel, check!"

"Jacket, check!"

"Safety belt, check!"

"Good to go!"

Minato moved on autopilot, equipping each piece without missing a beat. Then he grabbed an air tank and slung it over his shoulders. From start to finish, it only took him 45 seconds max. Once he was done, he ran off to the garage, leaving Wasabi behind. The order called for both a tiller truck *and* a pumper, so apparently this was one serious blaze.

Their sirens blared through the sleepy town.

"Apparently it was a large amount of commercial-grade fireworks that sparked the blaze," the lieutenant explained as he pulled on his fireproof gloves. Behind his glasses, the look in his eyes was grave.

Hinako waffled back and forth, carrying her most precious possession: her surfboard. She had experienced fire drills back in school, but this was her first time dealing with the real thing.

Just a few moments ago, she had snapped awake to the sound

of explosive fireworks as her balcony lit up like a summer day. Then she heard other residents screaming about a fire and immediately leapt out of bed.

She had wasted another day surfing, so her apartment was still nothing but piles of cardboard boxes. If a single spark found its way inside, it would all go up in flames...but this was no time for idle speculation! *Ugh, I should've unpacked like Mom told me to!*

"Okay, uh...phone!"

Hinako couldn't make a U-turn with a surfboard in her hands, so instead she walked backwards out of the valley between the boxes.

"Wee-woo, wee-woo! Fire! Fire!"

Yes, I've noticed! Thank you, Mr. Fire Alarm!

"Uhhh...wallet!" Right as Hinako returned with her phone, she remembered something else and had to rewind all over again.

In school she'd learned the "PuRCH" system—*no pushing, no running, no chatting, no heading back*—but naturally, during an actual crisis, it was the furthest thing from her mind. Humans could accomplish many incredible things during times of emergency, but evidently, thinking clearly wasn't one of them.

By the time Hinako finally made it out of her apartment, the hallway was filled with the smell of smoke. *Wait, is this actually a big fire? Crap, I'm on the eighth floor! I gotta get outside!*

"Aagh! Wait!"

But by the time Hinako made it to the elevator, it was already on its way down, carrying the other residents.

Wait, I know! The emergency stairs!

Hinako ran down the hallway and threw open the door to the stairwell. Smoke was rising from the lower floors...so if she couldn't go down, her only option was to go up. She dashed up the staircase without another thought.

Just five minutes after the first call to 119, the fire department arrived at the nearest hydrant. They lifted the cap with a crowbar, and sure enough, water sprang up. Next, they attached the hose.

"Deploy the water!"

Instantly, the pumper's hose puffed up, and it was time to lay siege to the burning stairwells and balconies. Meanwhile, fireworks erupted from the construction site next door.

"Target: sixth-floor external staircase! Connect to the fifth-floor integrated water supply pipe and deploy! Number Two, Number Three, get up there!" the squad captain commanded.

"Yes, sir!"

Number Two—that was Wasabi. Together, he and Number Three sprang into action.

"Up, up, up, up!"

Carrying the hose extension, they dashed up the emergency staircase to the fifth floor, where they connected it to the building's hose outlet.

"Deploy the water!"

It was time to put all that training to use.

Meanwhile, in the first floor lobby, another firefighter was busy getting a head count of the evacuated residents and checking for any missing or injured individuals.

"Stay calm, folks! I'm taking everyone's apartment numbers!"

"I forgot my teddyyyy!" a little girl wailed from the safety of her mother's arms. Her young parents must have been too flustered to think to grab their daughter's favorite toy.

Outside, the lieutenant called the shots from the fire car, passing along information and new orders to his subordinates. In other words, he served as the control tower for the operation.

"So far the fire hasn't made it inside, and the residents have evacuated to the first floor. One female eighth-floor resident noted missing. Number Two, Number Three, put that fire out and go find her!" he commanded into his lapel radio.

"Roger!"

Wasabi and the rest of the pumper squad still had no idea that the missing resident was, in fact, "Miss Hero."

Meanwhile, on the opposite side of the building, Minato was on the tiller truck, busily fighting the balcony fires. One of the residents had left some bundled magazines out on their balcony, which was where the blaze had initially begun. The whole balcony was burned black, the sliding glass door had melted, and the apartment interior was completely waterlogged. The balconies immediately above and below had suffered significant damage as well.

The truck's ladder could extend up to 100 feet, enabling Minato to perform rescues and extinguish fires from up close.

Once the balcony was fully extinguished, he maneuvered in close and lifted a wet and charred teddy bear from the ashes.

Pew, pew, pew! BOOM!

Up on the roof, Hinako had a front-row seat to her very own fireworks show. *Everything's flying so fast, you'd think there was a liquidation sale.*

"Aaah!" Hinako screamed as a shower of sparks rained down on her. *Thanks for the invite, but I'll pass!*

Carrying her surfboard like a turtle shell, Hinako crouched forward at a near right angle and ran to one corner of the roof, where she peeked over the edge. Down on the ground, she saw several fire trucks and plenty of firemen.

She took a deep breath and shouted: "Heeeelp!"

Behind her, another firework exploded with a deafening boom. Fortunately, a man in glasses noticed her and started talking into his radio.

They're gonna save me! Thank God! As sparks flew in every direction, Hinako crouched down under her surfboard and hunched her shoulders. Each passing second felt like an eternity. *Somebody, please, save me!*

"Are you all right?!"

Footsteps were coming up the stairwell. But before Hinako could rejoice, an even bigger firework went off directly behind her, and she whirled around.

A crane slowly reached in her direction. Behind it, neon fireworks bloomed like chrysanthemums. Hinako sucked in a breath.

There, in the bucket of the crane, was a young man with dark, almond-shaped eyes. He was smiling as if they were old friends, possibly in an attempt to reassure her.

"Are you all right?" His voice was pillowy soft.

"I...uh..." Slack-jawed, Hinako stared at his face. He was so handsome that he looked like a movie star. Swap the uniform and crane for a cape and a white horse, and you'd have Prince Charming! She might have swooned, you know, if the building wasn't literally on fire.

"Are you hurt?"

"No, I'm okay!"

Boom, boom, boom! The fireworks detonated one after another.

"Stay calm. I'm going to get you out of there." The man opened the bucket door, and Hinako timidly approached.

"Can I bring my surfboard with me?" she asked.

"Of course." He grabbed it from her with both hands. "It'll be a tight fit, but once you're on board, I need you to crouch down low."

Fearfully, she boarded the bucket, put on the helmet he handed her, and crouched down, just as instructed.

"Missing resident in custody!" the man called down. "Lower the crane!"

With a high-pitched whine, the crane began to descend, swooping like the long neck of a brachiosaurus.

Holy crap, we're so high up! Hinako wasn't especially afraid of heights, but regardless, she clung to the bucket railing.

There would be no surviving a fall from this height—not unless you were on the water. That was the biggest difference between land and sea. But the firefighter scarcely seemed to mind; he gazed at her with a confident smile. Seriously, why did he keep looking at her like he recognized her? Or was that familiarity just in her head?

Eventually the bucket touched down on the ground.

"You're safe now," said the firefighter as he handed Hinako's surfboard back to her.

"Thank you so much!" Not only had he saved Hinako's life, he had saved her *board*, which was worth just as much. She couldn't begin to express her gratitude.

"Don't worry about it," he said. "If anything, I should thank you."

Huh? What do you mean? But before Hinako could really think about it—

"Hinageshi! You know you're not allowed to bring personal property into the bucket!" the man in glasses shouted angrily.

"Sorry, sir!"

Wait, what? But you said it was okay! Hinako winced. "Sorry I got you in trouble."

"It's all right. That board means a lot to you, right?" he asked casually.

"Yeah, I've had it ever since I was a kid. Although it's practically falling apart..."

"I'd like to see you ride it again sometime."

"Huh?"

"Now and then I see you from the roof of the station. Out on the waves."

"Hinageshi! We're pulling out!" The bespectacled man was calling for the firefighter again.

The young man smiled stiffly and then raised his hand in farewell to Hinako. "See you around."

"Wait!" Hinako shouted reflexively. "If you're interested... uhh...would you want to...learn to ride? With me?" She made a "wave" motion with her hand. Looking back, it was a ballsy invitation, especially since she'd only just met the guy.

"Or do you already know how?" she added as an afterthought.

He responded by grinning from ear to ear.

Ride your Wave

CHAPTER 2
Takeoff

ROPE: A USEFUL TOOL in the business of saving lives. As such, all firefighters were required to participate in rope drills. Some drills involved climbing a rope to high places, and some, like the one Wasabi was currently doing, involved maneuvering over a rope bridge in order to cross rivers or gaps between buildings.

"Come on, come on, come on!"

These sixty-foot ropes extended from the main training building to the auxiliary training building. On the way out, the firefighters were instructed to climb sailor-style, and on their return trip, monkey-style. These names were rather apt; the former involved using both hands to pull one's body along the rope, like a sailor, and the latter involved hanging upside-down, like a monkey.

Another firefighter had started climbing at the same time as Wasabi, but he had already completed his round trip. Wasabi, however, had run into some trouble on his way back. They had performed this drill several times already, and he was starting to lose strength in his hands. Sailor-style wasn't too hard as long as you knew the trick to it, but monkey-style required a lot of upper-body strength and therefore was massively draining.

Unsurprisingly, Wasabi's hand slipped, and he plummeted headfirst toward the ground—or he would have, if not for the lifeline tied around his waist.

"What's the matter with you?!"

"Keep trying!"

As he hung upside down, his squad mates shouted words of encouragement. *Sorry, guys, but this is agony!*

"You can do it!"

"One more push!"

Damn it. Using his stomach muscles, Wasabi hauled himself upright and started to climb his lifeline up to the main rope.

"That's it! Don't be a quitter!"

Sweat streamed from his brow in a torrent, but he didn't have the energy to wipe it away. It took everything he had just to get back to the horizontal rope and grab it with both hands.

"Now your legs! Hook 'em on there!"

Wasabi got one leg on—but when he went to hook the other, he fell again. Every time he slipped, it crushed his spirits a little more, making it even harder to recover.

"You still got this! Don't give up!"

"Take a deep breath and try again!"

"Use your muscles! Grab on tight!"

He could tell their hearts were in the right place. Biting back the urge to vomit, Wasabi made another attempt...but he'd lost his grip strength entirely. His physical and mental energy were both exhausted. All he could do was dangle there and wait to be rescued.

Defeated, he let out a sigh.

Later, as Wasabi was throwing himself a silent pity party in the changing room, Minato walked in. "Nice work out there!"

"Very funny... I think maybe I'm not cut out for this job," Wasabi replied weakly without looking at him.

"Mistakes are no big deal. All you have to do is try harder next time."

Minato always made it sound so easy. Probably because he was the most talented firefighter on the force. Minato had also been the guy who climbed out to rescue Wasabi while he was dangling.

"It's not that simple, man," Wasabi muttered, staring up at the ceiling and trying not to cry. "I feel like I chose the wrong career."

"You know Koba-san, the driver engineer? Have you seen his mapwork?"

Koba was a veteran engineer who had recently transferred in from another town. His job: to drive the fire truck in a safe, speedy, and precise fashion, plus control all the truck mechanisms. And during the most recent fire outbreak, yes, Wasabi had seen the man's mapwork. Koba had only been at their station a few days, and yet he already knew which roads were blocked off, as well as the locations of all the hydrants, storage tanks, short-cuts, and water lines. Each day Koba added something new to his maps, all so the team would have this information when they needed it most.

"It's not easy to get to his level. It takes a lot of hard work and dedication. You're a brawny guy—I'm sure you'll be better than me in no time." Having changed into his street clothes, Minato offered Wasabi a pat on the back. Then he headed for the exit. "See ya!"

"Senpai!" Wasabi called reflexively, and Minato turned back. "What's got you in such a good mood?"

There was a skip in Minato's step. A glint in his eyes. Had something special happened?

"I'm gonna catch some waves." Grinning, Minato held up one hand with his thumb and pinky extended in a shaka and waved.

Hinako's college was located right on the water—so close that she could hear the ocean waves from the classroom. Given the sheer size of the campus, one could almost mistake it for a beach resort.

Mmmm, the weather's so nice today... Maybe I'll skip my after-noon classes and go surfing instead...

Hinako had only just enrolled, but already she was tempted to slack off.

Japan was an island nation surrounded by water on all sides, and yet for some reason only a select few colleges offered oceanography courses. Of course, "oceanography" covered a wide variety of fields: marine biology, nautical science, fisheries science, marine geology, marine engineering, ocean conservation, et cetera, et cetera. (For this reason, it was considered an "integrated interdisciplinary science" in Europe and North America.)

Because it was such a complicated field of study, all of Hinako's classmates had very specific ambitions for their future: working at an aquarium, being an oceanographer, stuff like that. Those who enrolled without putting much thought into it—like Hinako herself, who simply "loved the ocean"—were now paying the price. Who knew it would involve so many boring science classes? Especially chemistry. Ugh, what a nightmare.

If only Hinako had a boyfriend, she could spend her college days blissfully in love. But tragically, she had zero experience with boys... Well, except for that one time.

It had been her second year of high school, and over summer break, Hinako had spent her days surfing and working part-time at a seaside clubhouse. There, she met a college student—she couldn't remember what he looked like, but she remembered his gorgeous, expensive, top-of-the-line surfboard.

Oops, maybe *that* had been what she actually fell in love with. She had just been so naive back then...

(Never mind that this was only two years ago.)

But as it turned out, the surfboard—er, the college guy— hadn't actually known how to surf at all. He'd been what you might call a total poser. But Hinako hadn't looked down on him for it, though. After all, he could always learn. If anything, she just thought his lack of know-how was a terrible waste of a several-hundred-thousand-yen board...

And she *miiiight* have said that to his face too...

Regardless, when he found out she was a pro-level surfer, he got oddly upset and started hanging out with some other (non-surfer) girl who worked at the clubhouse next door instead.

And thus had Hinako said goodbye to her "surfer" "boyfriend" after a mere thirty-six hours.

But obviously that didn't really count, right? Maybe that was why the Goddess of Love had chosen to throw her a bone. Sure, the apartment fire had been a total nightmare—but without it, she never would have met the firefighter of her dreams.

Over the past few days they'd messaged back and forth via LINE chat, and even spoken over the phone on occasion... And tomorrow, on his day off, they would at last finally go surfing together.

It was a perfect sunny day, and a pleasant breeze blew in through the car window. That, plus the gentle vibrations of the engine, *plus* a critical lack of sleep, all combined to create one sleepy Hinako. Her eyelids drooped against her will.

"Should we have agreed on a later time?" the firefighter asked as he gripped the steering wheel. Today he was wearing a denim button-up over a plain cotton T-shirt. His work uniform was super sexy, of course, but he looked right at home in a more casual grunge style too.

"Oh, no, I'm wide awa—" But before Hinako could even finish her sentence, she felt a giant yawn coming on, so she hastily clapped a hand over her mouth. "Weird... Why am I yawning...?"

Not only had this outing been her suggestion, he'd gone to the trouble of picking her up in his car! Ugh, she was being so rude! Maybe all the excitement had fried her brain.

Fortunately, he was willing to laugh it off. "Feel free to nap until we get there. I know you had to move a lot of stuff."

He was just so mature and considerate—nothing like the guys her own age.

"Yeah, but all I had to do was carry it down a bunch of floors. Piece of cake!" Hinako said. *God, please don't let him find out my whole apartment was nothing but boxes.*

"The balconies at that complex are extremely flammable, so be careful. If a fire starts on a lower floor, it'll shoot up faster than you know it."

Come to think of it, the fire had mostly spread in a single vertical line.

"Got it! I'll be careful," said Hinako. *Note to self: keep the flammable stuff inside the house.*

"I gotta say, your job sounds pretty complicated," she added. "They were shooting off fireworks over in that half-finished building next door, right? And you guys had to set 'em straight?"

Apparently the source had been a group of rowdy young adults. They had trespassed into the construction site, and they hadn't had a pyrotechnics license either. Without that license, they couldn't legally purchase commercial-grade fireworks...so where had they gotten their hands on all that?

"Tell me about it. What a headache... Apparently it's some kind of new viral video challenge."

So they'd done it all for the views? But this stunt was far more serious than simply playing with sparklers in the park...and yet none of them had showed a trace of remorse while they were giving their statements to the police.

"I actually used to live in this area back when I was little," said Hinako. "But then we had to move closer to my grandparents so my dad could take over the family business...but I've always wanted to move back, y'know? So I enrolled at the college here."

The car flew breezily down Surf Street.

"So anyway, what about you, uhhh...insert-name-here?" she asked.

"What?"

Clutching her head, Hinako decided to just come clean. "Ugh, I'm sorry! I don't know how to pronounce your name!"

On LINE, the firefighter's user handle displayed 雛罌粟港— the sort of obscure *kanji* characters you'd see on a quiz show on TV.

"My last name? It's *Hinageshi*."

"Oh, so *that's* how you pronounce that?!" Come to think of it, Hinako remembered the man in glasses calling for "Hinageshi" the night of the fire. "So it's Hinageshi...Minato? Or...?"

"Yeah. A lot of people think it's *Kou*, but it's Minato."

"Oh yeah, I can relate. People always read my last name *Mukoumizu*, but it's actually Mukaimizu." And since *mukoumizu* carried the double meaning of "reckless," this misreading often felt like a stealth insult.

"Got it," Minato grinned, and Hinako swooned a little. "For the record, next time there's a fire, you want to try to get to low ground. Go down, not up."

Oh, okay. I'd better make another mental note.

Just then, Hinako looked up and spotted two plushie keychains hanging from the rearview mirror. One was a sea turtle, just like Minato's LINE icon, and the other was—

"Is that a finless porpoise?!"

"Sure is! And not a beluga, contrary to *most* people's assumptions," Minato nodded cheerfully.

"I knew it!"

This came as a surprise and a delight. Many people mistook Hinako's porpoise decal for a beluga. While the two animals did look similar at first glance, in reality they were actually *very* different in size. The finless porpoise was easily among the smallest species of whale.

"You must really like them. Even your car looks like a porpoise!" Hinako said. With its circular headlights and rounded frame, Minato's car looked exactly like a cartoony little porpoise. "I'm a big fan of porpoises, actually! They remind me of Bakeratta, you know?"

Bakeratta was a baby ghost from an old vintage anime who was shaped like an upside-down fishbowl. Technically his name wasn't Bakeratta—that was just the only word he knew how to say. But because of that, Hinako's family always referred to him as

Bakeratta. What was his actual name, again? He was Little Ghost Q-Taro's younger brother, so...Q-Taro II?

According to Minato, this cute little porpoise car was in fact a 1960s French compact economy model.

"Should I put on some tunes?" he asked. "What kind of music are you into?"

Hinako appreciated his casual segue. Meanwhile, they headed up the Tokyo Bay Aqua-Line from Kisarazu to Kawasaki.

"Just put on whatever music you like," she told him.

"Hmmm... Okay, then..." Minato connected his smartphone to the cassette adapter and pushed it into the player. A familiar upbeat melody began to play.

"Oh my God, what a throwback!" Hinako gasped.

It was a J-pop song by a well-known boy band. When Hinako was little, this song had topped all the charts. They'd played it all the time at the seaside clubhouse too.

"It got featured in a movie recently, so they're playing it on the radio again," said Minato.

Interesting. Evidently the two of them had the same taste in music. This won a lot of brownie points with Hinako.

I see you there, looking at the water
Glittering sapphire as far as the eye can see
Bit by bit, you'll find that its color will change
Kaleidoscopic majesty

But our lives won't always be sunshine

Now and then the rain will fall
And if you want to, you could just stand there
Or together we'll rise up and fight through it all

That's right
Now's the time to open your eyes and see
The start of your brand new story
The rest of your life is just around the bend
Just keep pushing forward and in the end
You'll find your way back to me
This is our story...

Just like that, Hinako was back in her comfort zone, and as she sang along happily, Minato smiled at her and joined in.

In order to teach a beginner surfer how to do a takeoff—i.e., the transition to a standing position on the board—you ideally wanted to start them off at a wide, shallow beach where it would be easier to read the waves. The size and condition of any given wave was subject to change depending on the wind and direction of said wave.

After spending the previous night thoroughly researching the weather reports and checking the wave conditions according to the local surf shops, Hinako settled on the Southern Beach Chigasaki in Kanagawa Prefecture for their destination. Of course, their local Kujukuri Beach back in Chiba Prefecture was a surfer's paradise in its own right—arguably even Japan's most preeminent surfing location, given the sheer number of waves it boasted—but at this time of year, the wind was unruly and the weather was unpredictable. (Admittedly, this extensive research was partially to blame for Hinako's lack of sleep.)

They pulled into the parking lot. Atop the car, Hinako's weathered old shortboard and Minato's brand-new longboard were nestled together like a couple of lovebirds.

"I see you went out and bought your own," Hinako commented. At a glance, she could tell he'd carefully chosen an affordable board appropriate for his height. And he had a porpoise decal too! While hers was a full-body porpoise, his was just the face, complete with an angelic little smile.

"I figured it would help motivate me to learn."

Minato unstrapped his board from the rack and pulled it down. The thing was twenty pounds and more than nine feet long, but he hefted it like it barely weighed an ounce. He seemed a bit on the lanky side compared to Hinako's mental image of a burly firefighter, but evidently he was in better shape than she thought.

"Besides, I've been wanting to put this surfboard rack to use."

That kinda made him sound like a poser, but Hinako appreciated his honesty.

Here in the springtime, the beach was practically empty on a weekday. Only a handful of surfers had awoken from their winter hibernation. Plus, the waves were only waist-high at most.

Perfect.

Once Hinako finished changing into her yellow bikini, she

stood outside the men's changing room and waited for Minato to return. And when he did...

"Whoa! A full wetsuit!"

Indeed, he was covered from head to toe in black neoprene rubber. Clearly, he was taking this very seriously.

"Dude, you look hot! You're gonna be a pro surfer in no time!"

Hinako threw up a shaka, and Minato scratched his head sheepishly.

Paddling: the foundation of surfing.

After Hinako's long lecture on the beach about proper surfing stances and the importance of aligning one's center of gravity with the board, they started by paddling their boards out into the water while lying on their bellies. Sink or swim, as they say.

Together, they floated side by side as Hinako taught Minato the essential steps of paddling. *Keep your head raised and look into the distance to maintain your balance. Make sure the board stays parallel to the water's surface.*

"Lift your chest up! Now paddle, paddle, paddle!"

Minato was a surprisingly fast learner; he quickly mastered the most efficient strokes. Straddling their boards, they waited in an empty spot for a wave to come.

At last, it was time to practice the takeoff. To do so, they needed to locate the wave's peak—the most powerful part, where the whitewater was located—and try to catch it. Hinako sat perfectly still, scanning the waves and giving instructions to Minato.

"Paddle, paddle, paddle, paddle! Then jump up onto your feet!"

"Whoa!"

"Paddle, paddle! Pull your legs in and bounce up!"

"Aack!"

Every time Minato tried to stand, he slipped and fell into the water instead. He was clearly trying his damnedest—or maybe he was just desperate. Floundering in the water, he moved both arms in sync, like a butterfly stroke, as he paddled.

"Paddle, paddle, paddle! All right, hop up! Stay balanced!"

"Gah!"

The waves continued to elude him. Sometimes he couldn't make the turn in time, while other times he failed to paddle hard enough.

"Good, good! Get up! You got it, you got it! I know you got it this time!"

Unfortunately, that was not the case. The wave slipped past Minato, and he splashed headfirst into the water. But for a first-timer, he was doing incredibly well. Even those with the most gifted of reflexes generally struggled with this first takeoff...but those who mastered it could master surfing itself.

Around noon, the pair returned to dry land, where Minato stripped off the top half of his wetsuit and gasped for breath.

"You okay?" Hinako asked, peering at his face.

"I'll...haah...try harder...haah...after lunch..."

He looked frustrated—a feeling she could understand, especially since he'd gone to all the trouble of buying his own board.

They sat there for a few minutes until Minato caught his breath; then he unloaded some stuff out of the car, including a portable camping stove and a kettle.

"I'll make us some coffee."

While they waited for the water to boil, Minato took out a portable coffee grinder and started grinding up some beans. Hinako could scarcely believe it.

"You grind your own beans?!" She'd only ever had canned coffee—or instant, if she was lucky. As he continued to grind away, a rich fragrance rose into the air. Hinako flared her nostrils, taking it in. "That smells incredible...!"

"I made this blend to complement the flavor of the sandwiches," Minato explained as he poured the coffee grounds into a filter. Then, as he poured the hot water on top, the grinds began to swell.

"Whoa...!"

"When you brew fresh coffee grounds, they release carbon dioxide, which causes them to expand, like so." Minato poured the water in a circular motion, starting from the center and slowly moving outwards.

"Seems complicated!"

Minato's skills and knowledge were on par with those of a professional barista. He poured the steaming hot coffee into a large mug and then handed it to Hinako.

Holy crap! The flavor's so much better than instant!

Next, Minato took out a carton of eggs and cracked them into a bowl. He added a little dashi soup stock and gently mixed it all together with a whisk. What was he making this time? He seemed to sense her curiosity.

"It's for egg sandwiches."

Minato pulled out a rectangular *tamagoyaki* frying pan and set it on the heat. The egg mixture sizzled as he poured it in. Then, once the edges started to bubble, he used a pair of chopsticks to stir it around, applying heat evenly. Meanwhile, he arranged four slices of bread side by side in a square and spread mustard and mayonnaise onto them.

What a multi-tasker! thought Hinako. "Hinageshi-san, you're so good at everything! Are you Superman or what?"

They were only four years apart. Would she be this competent at adulting once she made it to his age?

With a quick flip of his pan, Minato folded the eggs in half, then placed this thick rolled omelet onto one half of the bread. He flipped the other slices on top and then got to work cutting it all into finger sandwiches with his knife.

"Whoaaaa!" Hinako was completely wowed. *No way am I letting this guy see my sad attempt at omurice.*

Meanwhile, Minato explained that firefighters were required to be on standby at all times in case of emergencies and therefore cooked their own meals at the station instead of going out to eat.

Above them, a black kite screeched as it rode the updrafts in a lazy circle, like a surfer of the skies. Hinako sat and waited patiently, and soon the finger sandwiches were ready. She opened her mouth wide and took a huge bite of hers. Her eyes flew open. *Holy crap, this is incredible! The eggs are so fluffy! And the mustard goes with it perfectly!*

"Y'know, back when you saved me from the fire, I thought to myself, 'You're a total hero, Hinageshi-san,'" Hinako gushed through a mouthful of food.

"Nah, I'm nothing special," Minato replied with a sheepish smile. "And I'd like it if you called me Minato, because I'd like to call you Hinako."

Wha?! Hinako's face flushed red, all the way to her ears. After what he had just said to her, surely anyone would react the same way...or was it because it was coming from a guy like him? On second thought, maybe that was the bigger reason.

But it was right as she let her guard down that tragedy struck.

"WHOA!"

Out of nowhere, the kite swooped down and absconded with Hinako's sandwich like it was a baby bunny.

"My food!"

Behind them, a sign read *BEWARE OF KITES: WILL ATTACK ANYTHING THAT MOVES.*

Alas, Hinako only had eyes for Minato.

"I'm so sorry! If it wasn't for me, you could have picked a spot with bigger waves!"

Minato apologized profusely with his hands pressed down on the table. During their post-lunch practice, he had nailed all his takeoffs, but unfortunately he had failed to catch a single wave.

"There will always be another wave. All you have to do is keep trying!"

Minato looked up in surprise, and Hinako grinned at him.

"Besides, I'm glad we decided to come here," she said, "if only to visit this cool café!"

Minato had brought her to a little seaside café called Siren, which was run by an elderly couple. Their main specialty was coffee, and they offered a wide variety of brewing methods: drip, pour over, cold brew, French press, and so on. (Minato seemed very passionate about this, but truth be told, Hinako didn't really know the difference.)

Weren't "sirens" those...monsters? Spirits? From Greek mythology? The ones who lured sailors to their death with their beautiful singing? The symbol on the store sign depicted a woman with wings, and the interior design featured a nautical theme with classical music played quietly in the background, so as to not get in the way of conversation. In this café, the coffee was the siren, luring in the customers.

In addition to coffee, they also offered ginger ale, grape juice, plum onigiri, baguette sandwiches with ham and cheese—a simple and traditional menu, which Hinako could appreciate. On top of all that, the food and drink was transported by a small freight elevator called a dumbwaiter. Pretty cool.

They were seated on the second floor, overlooking the first, and when their pancakes arrived, they were stamped with the café's trademark siren symbol.

"I've been wanting to try this place for quite some time," Minato mused after they finished, gazing down over the railing at the first floor. "I like that they've got plenty of fire extinguishers behind the counter."

Then he realized what he said and hunched his shoulders in embarrassment.

That's *the first thing you noticed?* Hinako burst out laughing. "You know, Hinage—"

She stopped short and averted her eyes shyly. It felt silly to call him by his first name when they weren't even dating, but... *Eh, screw it.*

"As long as I'm with you, Minato-san, I feel like I'm in safe hands."

"You are," he nodded. He abruptly leaned forward across the table. "I'll always be there to help you...always!"

It was so sudden, Hinako couldn't help but startle back. The look in his eyes was so intense, it made her blush...

"Well, uh...we should probably get going!" she blurted as she jumped to her feet.

"Oh, okay..."

Breathe, Hinako, breathe! God, my face must be as red as a fire truck! Avoiding Minato's gaze, Hinako speedily loaded the tray with their dirty dishes.

"I'll take care of that," Minato offered as he rose from his chair.

No, no, no, no! I can't look at him point-blank or my heart will explode! In a full-blown panic, Hinako sped over to the dumbwaiter, tray in hand. "I've got it covered!"

"Wait! Don't!"

But Minato's flustered shout didn't register, and Hinako stuffed the tray in through the open doors.

Then she felt the tray plummet downwards—much lower than it should have.

Wait, what?

"AAAHH!"

Right as Hinako stuck her head into the empty elevator shaft, there was a deafening crash as the dishes shattered down below.

She hadn't noticed them lower the dumbwaiter...

"I'm so sorry!"

Hinako bowed so deeply that her forehead practically touched her knees. Now Minato was probably pissed at her... *God, kill me now! I've already dug my own grave—I might as well dig all the way to Brazil and start my life over! I'll dance the samba until I forget any of this ever happened!*

Fortunately, the owners were extremely forgiving, and when she offered to compensate them for their broken dishes, they declined.

"Don't worry about it. It's an old machine," said the wife, dressed in an apron.

"You from Tokyo?" asked the husband, wearing a white button-down shirt, a black vest, a bow tie, and a pair of round glasses.

"Chiba, actually," Hinako answered.

"You don't say!" The wife smiled, wrinkles creasing around her eyes.

"One of our former employees opened his own branch there. You oughta stop by sometime," said the husband as he handed Hinako a business card. Sure enough, the address wasn't too far from her town.

"Their equipment isn't *quite* so old," the wife laughed amicably, her salt-and-pepper ponytail swaying with the motions.

After one final apology, Hinako and Minato left the café. The sun had started to sink beneath the sea, and the beach was now completely deserted.

"I'd like to run a café of my own someday," Minato sighed. Evidently firefighting wasn't his only dream.

And then there's me: a total hot mess. Hinako mumbled, "I'm sorry for freaking out back there."

And not in a cute way, either—in a "chasing a stray cat barefoot down the street" kind of way. If only she could *stop* and *think* instead of losing her cool around the only guy who'd ever shown interest in her... But after how careless she'd been just now, there was no way he would want to be around her anymore...

Heartbroken, Hinako put her hands on her hips and let the sea breeze blow against her.

"Would you want to do this again sometime...?" Minato murmured.

What...? As Hinako stared at him in shock, he turned and looked at her.

"Go surfing, I mean? Well...not that I'm any good at it." Minato averted his gaze in defeat for a moment, then looked back at her. "Or we could get coffee again...or we could go somewhere else, or..."

"Huh?!"

Wait, so he...he...he...?! Is this...?!

"I, uh..."

I'm not reading too much into it, right?! He's asking for a second date?!

"Yeah!"

Cheeks burning, Hinako bowed her head like she was asking for a favor.

And so their love story began.

Spring was coming to an end, and the waves were at peace.

People can fall in love for no real reason...or so they say, anyway. But in Minato's case, it didn't apply. He had his reasons—firm, unshakable reasons.

He loved that Hinako was always laughing about something, that she loved the ocean, and that she was good at surfing. He loved her big, expressive brown eyes and her healthy, tanned skin. And he loved her personality—the way she could be quiet and attentive one minute and spontaneous the next. Nowhere was her good-natured optimism more evident than in the words she'd said to him at the café: *There will always be another wave. All you have to do is keep trying!*

He found her inability to cook and clean kind of adorable, as well as her desperate attempts to hide this from him...and the fact that she wasn't actually any good at hiding stuff either. In short, he was nuts about her. Head over heels. Absolutely besotted. Call it whatever you like—he was willing to admit it.

Following their day trip to Chigasaki, Minato and Hinako messaged each other daily, arranging dates whenever their free time lined up. Thinking back, the ocean had sparkled just a little bit brighter the day Minato watched her surf from the station roof... Maybe it had been a sign of things to come.

One day, Minato was on cooking duty in the kitchen when he received an email from Hinako, who was at school. When he opened it, he burst out laughing. He had just sent her a photo of himself and Wasabi prepping for dinner (they were having barbecue, for the record), and she had responded with a group photo of her and her friends.

"Who's that?" Wasabi asked, peering over Minato's shoulder at the phone screen with a frown.

But Minato didn't blame Wasabi for not recognizing her. The three college students had a palette of paint all over their faces, like some kind of surrealist Picasso portrait. Sandwiched in the middle, Hinako looked a little miffed; clearly her friends had seen her looking at Minato's email and decided to tease her a little.

The young woman in glasses was "Ai-chan," and the one with the dark hair was "Jun-chan." Both shared a class with Hinako, and both dearly loved to give her a hard time about her new boyfriend.

Still, she was clearly having a fun time at college, even if she *did* regularly complain about the coursework being too hard.

If only she realized her mere presence could light up a room...

Hinako was radiant, like a sunbeam, and Minato was crazy about her.

Spring was almost over, and the weather at Kujukuri Beach was getting hotter with each passing day. The surfers turned out in such large numbers, you'd have thought summer was already upon them.

On his days off, Minato waited for Hinako to get out of class, then picked her up and took her to the beach to go surfing. Over time, he had shown dramatic improvement on the water— possibly because Hinako was a good teacher, or possibly because he had the aptitude for it, but in reality, probably both.

Together, they paddled out to the open sea. A wave approached from directly ahead; Minato leaned his weight onto the nose of the board, submerging it under the water to pass under the wave. Then he brought it right back up again. Duck dive: mastered.

He was going to catch a wave. Any wave, even a little one.

He shifted to the front half of the board to accelerate. He loved the feeling of the wind against his face. Beneath him, a little porpoise glided through the water, popping up occasionally to say hi. Soon the sea turtles would climb ashore to lay their eggs.

Hinako had once called him a "total hero," but she was wrong. If anything, *she* was the real hero.

She swam up beside Minato and hopped over onto his board for some tandem surfing. Her skin smelled like the sea and the sun, and he wondered what it would be like to hold her in his arms.

—*You finally caught a wave.*

—*Yep. And we did it together.*

Their shakas did all the talking for them. Meanwhile, Hinako's empty surfboard floated alongside them, glittering like snow in the sunlight.

And that's the story of how my hero became my girlfriend... Although it seems she hasn't realized who she is yet.

Over summer break, Hinako got a part-time job working at a flower shop. She had no intention of going back to her parents' oceanless city during the height of surfing season, and she had even *less* intention of being away from Minato.

Three months had passed since their first date, and every day with him was so magical, she almost wondered if she was dreaming. But she didn't spend every single day surfing, obviously. On weekends, Minato would pick her up in the Bakeratta and take her someplace fun as a surprise—like a poppy garden with entire fields full of flowers, or an aquarium on a rainy day, or an airport with flashing lights at night, or a spa resort with a neon fountain show.

On every drive, they always ended up listening to the same song they had played on their first surfing trip: *Brand New Story*.

They sang the lyrics so much, the rearview mirror plushies were probably sick to death of it. Sometimes they went out for mega-double-cheeseburgers, and one time Minato even took her on a surprise motor paragliding date!

But truth be told, Hinako didn't really care where they went. What made her happiest of all was simply the opportunity to share these little moments with Minato, be they pretty views, tasty food, jokes, or surprises.

One day found them driving along the coast of the Boso Peninsula to one specific beach famous for its gently sloping shores and beautiful sunsets.

"C'mon, hurry!"

Hinako ran down the wooden pier that extended into the ocean. Sundown was just a few moments away, and the sun was nearly about to kiss the horizon.

Holding hands, they sat down at the very edge of the pier. The sky was a brilliant blend of scarlet and burnt orange. In the distance, Mt. Fuji was slowly turning to shadow. All that surrounded them were gentle waves, ebbing and flowing.

The air was full of so much love, it drowned out the need for words. Their fingers entwined to match their hearts. Hinako had nothing to say—all she needed was the hand wrapped around hers. As the sun finally sank beneath the horizon, their lips were drawn together, like magnets.

It was their first kiss, and in that moment, Hinako was the happiest girl in the world.

As far as boyfriends went, Minato was flawless from every angle, like a 24-karat diamond. He was completely out of Hinako's league, and if she let him slip away, she'd never find another man as good as him—according to Jun and Ai, anyway. Of course, Hinako knew this all too well...but that didn't mean their relationship was totally perfect...

"This flower shop guy is so hot!"

"I know, right?!"

As Hinako was trimming the plant stems, a group of yukata-clad girls came into the store and crowded around Minato.

"I don't actually work here," he replied, looking perplexed.

But Hinako found herself wishing he would've been a bit more specific, like, *Sorry but I'm waiting for my* girlfriend *to get off work.*

"Where are you from?"

"We're going to see the fireworks after this. Would you wanna come with us?"

This was Hinako's biggest problem. Whenever she took her eyes off Minato for five seconds—even in the middle of a date—girls would surround him like moths drawn to a flame. She couldn't even run to the restroom in peace!

"Sorry, but I already have plans," said Minato.

Yeah, with your girlfriend! *You're letting them down too gently!*

Scowling, Hinako tried to focus on her work...but then she caught sight of her own face in the reflection of the glass.

Hmmm... Maybe I need to chill out.

In the reflection, she could see the girls behind her in their pretty yukatas, with their full makeup, perfectly styled hair, and painted nails. They had all put serious effort into their appearance. This made their red, swollen feet all the more adorably pitiful.

But then there's me...

Damaged hair from the salt water and UV rays (hence she wore it in a bun all the time). No makeup, just sunscreen. No girly outfits, either—most days she rocked a T-shirt, shorts, and flip-flops. But just because Minato was understanding, it didn't mean she was allowed to be lazy! Belatedly, Hinako realized just how little effort she'd put into taking care of herself.

A few days later, Hinako and Minato donned yukatas of their own to attend a different fireworks festival. Minato was wearing a striped yukata with a bucket hat—casual, yet stylish. Hinako had done her best to dress up too, following instructional videos online (although the bow in the back was just a clip-on).

But for the first time, she learned just how fun it could be to dress up for the man she loved...and the accomplishment she felt when he called her beautiful.

That summer was a summer of surfing. Hinako and Minato spent all their free time out on the water, riding countless waves. Then autumn started to take root, and right as Hinako swapped out her bikini and bun for a wetsuit with her hair down, Minato's twenty-third birthday rolled around.

"Happy birthday!"

They brought a cake to a karaoke room and celebrated together, just the two of them. The cake had frosting shaped like waves and a little chocolate plaque in the shape of a surfer, and believe it or not, it was *homemade*—okay, no, it wasn't. But it *was* custom-ordered from the bakery, and Hinako paid for it herself.

"Tadaaaa!"

The next thing she pulled out was a giant plastic porpoise— the inflatable kind, big enough that two people could have curled up inside it.

"It's huge!"

Sure enough, Minato loved it. But he only had himself to thank, because he was the one who'd taught Hinako how amazing it felt to have someone special put their heart and soul into planning the perfect gift. To commemorate the moment, they took a picture of themselves with the porpoise squished between them.

Hinako's next gift to Minato was a pair of matching smartphone covers. When pressed together from the side, they formed a single smiling porpoise. That way, even when they were apart, they'd always be together! Okay, maybe that was a melodramatic way to put it. But still.

Minato put their song into the karaoke machine and sang passionately while accompanying himself on a ukulele. Hinako hadn't even known he could play the ukulele!

Over the past six months together, Hinako had learned so much about Minato: his love of surprises, his competitive side, the way he laughed when something tickled his funny bone just right... Oh, and he hated broccoli—but because he was so stubborn, he always ate it anyway. What a dweeb.

Happy birthday, Minato. There's still so much more I want to learn...about you, and about love.

"So first you do *this*..." Minato carved out a hole in the center of a chocolate cupcake and then poured espresso into the cavity. "Now try it." Meanwhile, he popped the slender cylinder of cake into his mouth.

Hinako took a bite of the remaining cupcake, and her eyes flew open. The bitterness of the espresso had mellowed out the sweetness of the chocolate. It was the perfect balance!

"You're right! It really cuts the sweetness!"

As they grinned at each other, a teenage girl sitting at the table with them grumbled. "Good, because you two are *sickeningly sweet* as it is."

"I'm sorry my sister's so catty," Minato apologized.

Indeed, this was none other than Minato's younger sister Youko, currently in her second year of high school. She wore a duffel coat and low pigtails, and she was a pretty girl. Her pensive, almond-shaped eyes matched her brother's perfectly—

"Don't apologize for me, Oniichan!"

—except for when she glared.

"And bullheaded," Minato continued.

That much was obvious at a glance. Youko was still wearing her coat over her school uniform, which suggested that she wasn't planning on sticking around.

"Yeah, but I think we'll get along!" Hinako declared with a smile.

"Oh, do you?!"

"*Catty and bullheaded* is exactly how I'd describe my two best friends: Jun-chan the Scorpion and Ai-chan the Cobra!" Hinako showed Youko a photo of the three of them together.

"Why do they have such stupid nicknames?" Youko asked, brow furrowed.

"What would my sister be? Let's see... How about a blue-ringed octopus?" Minato suggested.

"An *octopus*?!"

"It may be small, but its bite contains a powerful neurotoxin called tetrodotoxin," he continued, wiggling his fingers like tentacles.

"Your brother sure knows a lot of stuff, huh?" Hinako grinned, gazing at Minato.

"I'm *leaving*," Youko spat as she rose to her feet. "I only came here to see what kind of girl you're dating, and now I've got my answer!"

"And what 'answer' would that be?"

"Dating is for squares! Now if you'll excuse me, this *blue-ringed octopus* is taking her neurotoxins and going home! Bye!" And with that, Youko grabbed her book bag and started to leave.

"Well, uh... Let's hang out again sometime, Youko-chan!" Hinako called after her, waving both hands.

Youko whirled around, glaring daggers. "Excuse me?!"

"I've built up an immunity to your poison, so I'll be fine!" Hinako cheerfully threw up a shaka.

"Forget it! Hmph!" And with that, Youko stormed out.

"I really appreciate you taking that in stride," Minato commented softly, gazing into Hinako's eyes. "My sister has a lot of trouble making friends, you know, with the way she is, and she used to skip school for weeks at a time. But lately she's been going again."

"Gotcha," Hinako replied with a soft smile. It was obvious just how worried Minato was for her, and how deeply he cared.

"So yeah, it'd mean a lot if you could be a friend to her."

"Of course!"

Sure, Youko had complained the whole time she was with them, but she *had* shown up, and she *had* finished her coffee. Besides, Hinako was a younger sister herself, so she could relate.

We may deny it, but at the end of the day, our big brothers mean the world to us.

It was Hinako and Minato's first Christmas Eve together, and they went to Chiba Port Tower. Something about the mirrored glass made it feel super sci-fi.

"Ooh!"

They were walking along, hand in hand, when Hinako suddenly took off running.

"Look! Mt. Fuji! You can see Mt. Fuji!"

Across Tokyo Bay, far in the distance, Mt. Fuji's peak glowed orange in the sunset—awe-inspiringly beautiful. As Hinako snapped some pictures on her smartphone, a jazzy tune suddenly started to play, and when they turned back to look, they found the tower exterior lit up in the shape of a Christmas tree, all the way to the top.

"Wow!"

At over 300 feet tall and 100 feet wide, it was one of the nation's largest LED Christmas trees. As the night drew on, crowds of families and couples would flock to it. Right as the couple were about to enter the tower, however, a voice rang out over the loudspeaker:

"Here's a message from Namikoshi Shouta-san to Uchida Mai-san: Merry Christmas! Let's spend the rest of our lives together. Will you marry me?"

Near the doors, a man knelt before his shocked girlfriend, holding up a bouquet of flowers in her direction.

A public proposal!

The crowd of onlookers broke into applause.

"Awww, that's so sweet!" Hinako exclaimed.

"I guess," Minato replied coolly. "Apparently you can arrange in advance to have them read out a message for you. Wanna go to the top?"

The next message was from a woman to her mother. Meanwhile, Hinako and Minato rode the glass elevator all the way to the top floor, 300 feet off the ground.

"It's so pretty!"

One by one, lights clicked on all over Tokyo Bay—the Ferris wheel at Kasai Rinkai Park, the whimsical factories at the Port of Chiba, the diamond-studded cityscape, the river of traffic lights... The view from the tower observation deck was so far beyond Hinako's expectations, it took her breath away.

"Think we can see Katamiya from here?" Hinako mused. Then she stopped short. "Oh gosh."

On the wall was a heart-shaped plaque that read *Lovers' Sanctuary*. Dozens of little heart-shaped message cards were pinned around it, each bearing a brief handwritten message—usually "I love you" plus the names of the couple who wrote it. But some were confessions of one-sided feelings, or vows of eternal love, or prayers for good health. This single wall contained countless untold hopes and dreams.

"Wanna write one?" Minato suggested.

"What? No way! I wouldn't even know what to put!" Hinako protested. *Plus, it's kind of embarrassing...*

"Oh, I get it," Minato teased. "You don't know how to write my name in *kanji*."

"Yes I do!" Hinako shot back, pouting.

"Okay then, let's see it." Minato held out a message card from behind his back. When had he grabbed that?!

Reluctantly, Hinako picked up a Sharpie. On the right side, she wrote her name in kanji: *Mukaimizu Hinako*. And on the left side...

"Well?" Minato pressed.

Rrrgh! Don't make fun of me!

There was a pause, and then...Hinako gave up and wrote his surname phonetically instead. But at the very least, she remembered the kanji for Minato!

"Your last name is just too complicated!" she complained with a scowl.

"Well, you'd better figure it out before it's *your* last name." And with that, Minato took their message card from Hinako and walked off.

"Huh...? Wha?" What was *that* supposed to mean?

But Minato didn't notice Hinako's confusion. Instead, he whistled their song as he pinned the message card among its siblings.

"Uh, hello?" Hinako pressed.

"Looks like they're lining up for photos," he said suddenly, gesturing to the photo op station.

Ugh, he's ignoring me! You can't just drop a line like that and walk off! It's not fair!

"There we are! What a great shot. You two look perfect together," said the photographer to the couple whose picture he was taking. "Yes, perfect! Let's get one more... All right, all done. Next!"

On the wall was an illumination in the shape of angel wings. Each couple stood in front of it, making it appear as if they themselves had grown wings. Totally #instaworthy, but the line was ginormous.

"Hinako, over here!" Just then, Minako beckoned her over. "C'mere a sec."

The angel wing lights were visible in the reflection of the glass windows, and if they positioned themselves just so, they could achieve pretty much the exact same effect...although they would be almost entirely in silhouette, but whatever. With the night-scape in the background, the alternative framing made them look all the more as if they had taken flight.

As Minato snapped a pic, Hinako glanced down and noticed that the hand railings near the windows were *covered* in heart-shaped padlocks. This was another popular attraction here at the Lovers' Sanctuary; like the message cards, the padlocks featured couples' names and short, affectionate messages. But right as she crouched down to admire them...

"Here."

Minato took a padlock out from behind his back, like some kind of magic trick. It felt like he was always two steps ahead of her. He must've said all that stuff on purpose to get her to write the message card too!

They wrote their names on the lock and then snapped it onto the railing. Maybe next time, when they came back to take it off, there'd be a ring on her finger... As Hinako fantasized about the prospect, a glint of white caught her eye through the window.

"It's snowing!"

No wonder it was so cold! There was no wind tonight, either—maybe it would stick.

"Uggghhh... I wish I didn't have to work tomorrow. It's Christmas!" But Hinako's boss had *begged* her to come in, just until noon, and she hadn't had the heart to say no. "They say that a big wave always comes the morning after the snow falls...and if you can catch it, your wish will come true. But I've never had the chance to try."

"Interesting..." murmured Minato.

Hand in hand, they watched as the snow continued to fall.

And so a White Christmas arrived.

Hinako and Minato had the campsite all to themselves; evidently they were the only two nutjobs willing to camp outside in the middle of winter. Once again, Minato showed off his Superman skills by pitching a tent, setting up the camping stove, brewing some coffee (with fresh grounds, of course), and making dinner. This was all done with his personal equipment, and he had everything they could possibly need.

On the menu for tonight, per Hinako's request, was omurice. Minato placed the perfectly oval omelet atop the chicken pilaf and then used a knife to slice it open. Eggy goodness oozed all over the plate.

"Amazing!" Hinako clapped excitedly as she crouched nearby, watching him work. "What's the trick to getting it to stay on top?"

"You need the outside firm but the inside soft," Minato explained as he set about frying up the second omelet. He looked like a hotel chef, clapping his wrist to flip the pan. "You want it to be just pliable enough to stay put. See? Like this." As he spoke, he rolled it around in the pan. "Wanna try?"

"Okay!"

Surely even Hinako could at least *place* the omelet correctly, right? Using her chopsticks, she gently, gently set it onto the rice—*There!*

Moments later, it rolled off again.

"Aagh!"

"Don't panic. You can still—oof..."

As Hinako attempted to use the side of the frying pan to lift it up again, it fell apart. Once again, she had turned an omelet into scrambled eggs.

Then it started to snow again. It was so cold, their breath left their lips in a white fog...and yet neither of them really seemed to mind.

"You sure this is what you want? Omurice for Christmas?"

"Yep! Ever since I was little, omurice was always my favorite treat."

And tonight's omurice was special, because Minato had written "Merry Xmas" on it in ketchup.

"Besides...I wanted to be alone with you," Hinako said. *That way we can do* this.

"Isn't it kind of hard to eat with one hand?" Minato laughed.

Indeed, Hinako's right hand was currently laced with Minato's left. This was another of her requests.

"Nope! I've been practicing. That way I can always hold hands with you, even when we're eating. I don't want to let go of you for a single second!"

"Then would you wanna move in together? Because I'm planning to move out of my parents' house," Minato replied casually.

"Careful! I might actually take you up on that!" *So if you were just joking, then you'd better admit it quick!*

"Sounds good to me. How soon are we talking?"

"What?!" For a moment, Hinako was speechless. *I should've known Minato wouldn't joke about this stuff!*

"Well...not right away," she continued awkwardly.

Minato rubbed his thumb against hers, encouraging her to speak her mind.

Yeah...I may as well be completely open with you. Hinako stared intently into the falling snow. "Once I learn to...ride my own wave... Right now I'm constantly dependent on you, but eventually I have to get in control of my own life, you know? I want to find my passion, like you have."

That way the two of them could stand on even ground. It was Minato's influence that had inspired her to start thinking about more than just the ocean.

"You're naturally good at a lot of things, so I'm sure you'll find it fast," Minato replied. "Me, though? I was always kinda useless."

"You expect me to believe that?" Hinako scowled. If Minato was "useless," then what did that make *her*?

"When I was a kid, I almost drowned out in the ocean. But someone saved me. I remember it all like it was yesterday," he explained slowly, gazing straight ahead. "I wanted so badly to be good at everything, but no matter what I tried, I always screwed up. Then one day, purely by chance, I spotted some baby sea turtles hatching on the beach."

"Sea turtles?"

"Haven't you seen the signboard about the sea turtle spawning grounds? Or have you not read it?"

Each year, from June to mid-August, an endangered species known as the loggerhead sea turtle came to lay their eggs at the beaches of Ichinomiya—including Kujukuri. Then, approximately two months later, the baby turtles hatched from their eggs and spent up to a full week clawing their way to the surface. But not all succeeded, and some died as a result.

Minato saw these baby turtles for the first time when he was still in elementary school. At the time, he was accompanying his grandfather, who was volunteering for a sea turtle conservation organization.

"Whoa, what the?!" he had exclaimed as dozens of tiny turtles came crawling up from underground. No one had instructed them to do this, and yet they flailed their little limbs, struggling desperately to get to the ocean. Their mother was nowhere to be seen. No matter how many times the waves pushed them back ashore, they kept trying again and again...because their little lives depended on it.

"When I saw those baby turtles fighting tooth and nail to get out there, I thought to myself: *I need to be like that*. So I started going with Grandpa on his beach patrols, and bit by bit, it led me to where I am now. I wanted to work in a field where I could help people."

"Ugh, you're so incredible..." Hinako leaned back so far that she nearly fell off her chair, and Minato swiftly propped her back up again. "I don't think I could ever be of help to other people. I have enough trouble dealing with my *own* problems! And even then, I can't solve them by myself! But then there's you...the guy who can do anything."

Hinako's words were laced with self-deprecation, frustration, and a tiny hint of envy. "Someone as perfect as you couldn't possibly know how it feels to be me. I can't even put an omelet on a bed of rice! I must look like such an idiot to you."

She knew she shouldn't take her frustrations out on him... and especially not on Christmas Eve...but she couldn't stop herself. Luckily, Minato didn't seem to mind.

"You say I'm perfect, but I can't ride the waves like you can." He smiled like it was no big deal. "Just think of your life like it's the ocean. Swim for a while, take breaks when you need to, and once you're rested up, get back out there. I'll be the harbor you come home to, so just call for me whenever you need to get away from it all."

As he spoke, he threw up a shaka.

How long is he going to keep coddling me like this? Hinako thought. His kindness stung a bit.

"How long do I have until you get sick of me?" she asked, smiling sadly.

"I'll be with you as long as it takes," he told her, gently cupping her face in his warm hands. "Whether that's ten years, twenty years...or until you're a little old lady."

And then he gave her the world's softest, sweetest kiss.

"I see you there, looking at the water… Glittering sapphire as far as the eye can see…"

Singing to herself, Hinako stepped outside the flower shop, carrying a wooden planter box. Even in the middle of winter, this store was still every bit as vibrant as spring, with blooms in every color of the rainbow. Roses, dahlias, black hellebores, flannel flowers—all of them winter darlings. But on Christmas, the leading lady was the poinsettia, naturally.

Brrrr! Hinako exhaled against her numbed fingers. She didn't mind getting up early, and she wasn't opposed to manual labor, but she really couldn't stand working with water during the winter, especially on mornings as chilly as this one. Nothing made her lose feeling in her fingers quite as fast as trimming the stems on the cut flowers.

As the sun peeked out over the horizon, the ocean was the first to warm up. Steam rose from the sand with each lapping wave.

This reminded Hinako: earlier, she'd noticed some men in Santa Claus outfits riding water scooters out there. She wasn't sure it was safe, since the waves were pretty hefty this morning, so she hoped they were taking precautions. *And please tell me they're not drunk.*

Just then, her phone beeped, letting her know she'd received a LINE message. She pulled her phone out of the pocket of her apron; it was from Minato. The two of them had only just parted ways an hour ago, and she seemed to remember him saying he was headed home to sleep, since he wasn't scheduled to work today...

"Wait...*what*?! Are you serious?!"

Gonna ride some waves. BBL.

"You're going without me?! That's not *fair*, you jerk!" Hinako shouted before she could stop herself. She was already trying not to look at the ocean so she wouldn't be tempted, and he'd just made it a hundred times worse!

She imagined him surfing the curl, zipping through the barrel at the speed of light, and then doing a bottom turn back up to the lip...his silhouette soaring through the morning air... *Augh, I'm so pumped now! Knowing him, he might even pull off an air reverse!*

She could picture Minato walking back onto dry land, steam rising from every inch of his body, sighing in satisfaction.

Rrrrgh, you lucky jerk! I wanna do some tube riding too! I swear, the second I clock out, I'm going straight to the beach! I've only got two hours left here—so you better wait for me!

"Nngh!"

Hinako hoisted up a heavy flower bucket—and the handles snapped off. The bucket hit the ground with a clang, spilling flowers and soil everywhere.

"Uggghhh..."

Never in Hinako's wildest dreams did she imagine this would turn out to be a bad omen.

"God, Minato! I can't believe you would go without me!"

After dashing home to change into her wetsuit, Hinako raced on her bicycle all the way to the beach.

"Huh?"

There, on the snow-laden beach, was a red fire truck—but not the same one she recognized from the fire. Was that...a search and rescue truck? And an ambulance? And a patrol car?

Next to them sat Minato's Bakeratta, alone and forgotten, like a dog waiting for its owner.

Hinako's heart fluttered in her chest.

Parking her bicycle next to the Bakeratta, she walked across the beach, surfboard in hand. Her heartbeat pounded in her ears. She could see three water scooters sitting by the water's edge...and a whole team of rescue workers...and a rescue boat out on the water.

That's weird... Why is my sight getting all blurry?

Three young men stood on the beach. One of them was wrapped up in a blanket, while the other two hung their heads. All of them wore Santa Claus outfits, and Hinako recognized them as the same three men she'd seen earlier that morning.

Then...who are they searching for?

The temperature was freezing, yet a cold sweat trickled down her back.

A diver with an air tank jumped backwards off the rubber rescue boat into the water.

Staggering along the shore, Hinako noticed the front half of a surfboard floating aimlessly with the waves.

A surfboard with a porpoise decal...

"Hinako-san!"

Who's calling me?

"HINAKO-SAN!"

But the next thing she knew, everything went dark.

Ride your Wave

CHAPTER 3
Damping

Hinako couldn't really tell if she was awake or asleep. She couldn't recall the last time she ate. Then again, she didn't feel hungry.

She'd never thought there would come a day that she *wouldn't* want to be at the beach. But no, she didn't want to leave her apartment at all. She didn't have the energy. Instead, she hid indoors like she was allergic to the sun.

While she was awake, her brain replayed scenes from her time with Minato, over and over and over, like a broken projector. When she closed her eyes, she could see it all from a third-person perspective, like she was watching a movie.

It started at the end of summer—Hinako running barefoot across the beach, Minato chasing after her. Then he pulled her into his arms and swung her around as the waves sparkled behind them. Both grinned from ear to ear.

Then autumn descended over the beach. A close-up of the happy couple feeding the seagulls. The camera panned to the ocean and zoomed in on the couple in their wetsuits, lying side by side on their surfboards, holding hands and chatting.

Then the sparkling ocean transitioned to Christmas lights, revealing a theme park in winter. Hinako and Minato walked through the park, gazing up at the paper lanterns, holding hands, and wearing matching knit caps. Minato went in for a kiss, but Hinako bashfully deflected it with her hand. He waited for her to let her guard down and then went for it again. Their romance was as sweet as candy.

The final scene took place between the bedsheets, on the morning after Hinako's birthday. *I love you,* Minato whispered, affectionately gazing down at her from above. *I love you too,* Hinako replied, cupping his face in her hands. They kissed again and again.

But this movie had no ending. And it never would.

Had Hinako ever really kissed his lips? Or felt his body heat? Had she ever truly been that happy? It all felt fake. She'd thought she had known everything about Minato, but she never realized he was a bad swimmer. And now, just like that, he was gone. Had he ever really been there? Or had her brain simply invented the perfect man?

Just when Hinako thought she was finally out of tears, her eyes burned all over again. This could have been a neat party trick if it were something useful, like holy water or crude oil, but her unending fountain of tears did nothing to ease the agony in her chest.

Hinako's phone rang atop the table where she'd left it. After two rings, her voice mail answered for her. "The number you have dialed is unavailable or not in service at this time. Please leave a message after the tone."

Beeeep.

"Hinako?"

It was her mother. Clutching at her hair, Hinako sat among the cardboard boxes, her knees tucked up to her chin.

"How are you feeling, sweetheart? Give me a call when you're ready. You can take as much time as you need."

Hinako knew her family was worried about her, since she hadn't gone back to visit them for New Year's. But right now, their concern was smothering. She rubbed her big toes together.

"Message received on the 16th at 2:42 PM," the automated message finished.

Sixteenth? Of what month?

Time had stopped for Hinako on that fateful day.

THank Xuo fon SaVeing My TeDDy!! -YOShiKaWa YuuKi

At the station, Wasabi sniffled as he read a clumsily written letter addressed to Minato from a child whose toy Minato had recovered during the fire at Hinako's apartment complex. Enclosed with the letter were a few pictures: one of the kid with her slightly burnt buddy, and some of her dressed up as a firefighter and holding a hose at what appeared to be a children's career-themed amusement park.

Oh, I see. Minato-senpai inspired you, didn't he? Wasabi smiled slightly and glanced over at the empty desk adorned with flowers, drinks, and snacks. His personal contribution: a small sea turtle plushie. Additionally, there was a framed photo of Minato giving a firm salute in his firefighting gear. Even Wasabi could tell it was a swoon-worthy shot.

It was still so hard to believe he was gone.

Being a firefighter meant coming face-to-face with death every day. It was a dangerous job, and sometimes saving lives meant risking your own. Obviously Wasabi understood that by now, but...

"Hey there!" a voice called out from the doorway.

"Oh..."

Wasabi looked up and saw Youko standing there, wearing a duffel coat over her uniform.

Youko pressed the doorbell—ding-dong. No response.

She pressed it again—ding-dong, ding-dong. No response.

Dingdongdingdongdingdongdingdongdingdong! She mashed it stubbornly, as if to suggest she wasn't going to stop until the door opened. Wasabi stood behind her, carrying a cardboard box.

Bam, bam, bam! Having lost her patience, Youko started pounding on the door with her fist. "Hello? I know you're in there! Open the door, please!"

A few moments later, the door finally opened, and Hinako appeared, looking haggard. This was the first Wasabi had seen of her since Christmas, when she passed out on the beach. Her gait was unsteady—maybe her blood sugar was low.

"Sorry to drop in on you with no warning," Wasabi apologized sheepishly once they were inside her apartment. "I see you moved away from the coast, huh?"

Hinako's new place was located on the riverside instead.

"I figured this way I wouldn't have to look at the ocean," she murmured.

"Oh." Like an idiot, Wasabi had inadvertently reminded her of her dead boyfriend.

"This is all the stuff Oniichan left behind at the fire station," Youko continued sharply. "Do you need any of this crap or what?"

When Hinako saw the item sitting on top of the pile, her expression twisted in misery. It was the plastic inflatable porpoise, deflated and neatly folded up. Wasabi remembered Minato telling him Hinako had given it to him as a birthday present.

"I...I'm really sorry about this. I know it probably...brings up a lot of memories..." Tears spilled from Wasabi's eyes. He felt the same pain Hinako did—the pain of losing a loved one.

"We didn't come here so *you* could cry," Youko snapped.

But Wasabi couldn't stop. "I can't help it! I mean, they sent me out to rescue my own coworker... Can you even imagine...?"

On Christmas morning, Minato had gone out surfing alone. According to the young male witnesses who were riding their water scooters at the time, he was performing stunts and turns like a total pro. When one of the scooters capsized, he had already gone ashore, but then he heard the other two calling for help and ran back into the water with his board.

The young men were locals, and they knew the Kujukuri waves were not to be taken lightly, so they'd been hesitant to dive under the water to rescue their friend. Not only that, they'd been hungover from binge drinking the previous night. Nevertheless, they had gone out on the water.

But Minato plunged into the ocean regardless. He had never mastered water rescue training, but it was a firefighter's duty to help people in need.

The young man was almost unconscious by the time Minato got him onto his surfboard, and they were headed back to the shore when tragedy struck.

"In the end, he sacrificed his own life for someone else's... That's just the kind of man he was..."

"No! You don't understand!" Hinako shot back. "It's all my fault... I told him the waves got bigger the morning after a snowy night!"

"Stop it!" Youko shouted. "Blaming yourself isn't going to bring my brother back!"

The words seemed to hit Hinako like a ton of bricks. She stared at the floor. "I'm sorry... I'm so sorry..."

"Here's his cell phone." Scowling, Youko dropped the phone on top of the open cardboard box. "All this crap is yours now, so you can do whatever you want with it. Hell, throw it away if you want."

"Youko-chan!" Wasabi shouted, flustered.

"It's for her own good!" Youko shouted back as Hinako continued to hang her head. Then she jumped to her feet and stormed out.

"Um... Let me give you my contact information. If you ever need any help with anything, give me a call." Wasabi scribbled his cell phone number onto the back of his business card and placed it on Hinako's floor. Then he ran out of the apartment after Youko.

With Wasabi and Youko gone, the apartment fell silent once more.

Hinako reached out and gently ran a finger over Minato's phone screen. It was smooth and cold—no trace of its owner's warmth. She picked it up and flipped it over to look at the phone case. Half of a porpoise smiled up at her.

At one point, Minato had taught her about a smartphone app he'd discovered.

"Have you heard of this wave forecast app?"

"What?! I didn't know they made an app for that!"

The app provided a map of the coast, complete with markers and detailed status information. This way, the user could tell at a glance which spots had the best waves—insanely useful for a surfer.

"Here, I'll install it on your phone for you."

Hinako could remember him smirking as he put his arm around her shoulder...

She set his phone down and then used her own phone to call his number. Sure enough, his phone began to buzz.

Normally, Minato answered after a few rings. She could remember the sound of his voice calling her name. But instead, a mechanical voice answered coldly in his place: "The number you have dialed is unavailable or not in service at this time."

Why? Why*?!* Fury rose up inside Hinako, and she raised her phone high in the air—

"Please leave a message after the..."

She stopped herself. Instead, she lowered her phone and screamed into it: "You said you'd always be there for me, and now you're *unavailable*?! Screw you!"

But no amount of screaming would reach Minato now.

Beside Hinako, someone was on their board doing a takeoff. Someone in a wetsuit. She recognized him even from behind—

"Minato?"

But the moment she called out to him, he disappeared under the waves.

Instantly, Hinako snapped awake. Apparently she'd nodded off at some point. Silently, she cursed herself for waking up. If only she could've stayed in that dream world a little longer...

Then she realized she'd fallen asleep on the floor, on top of the deflated porpoise. Minato's other belongings from the box—his ballpoint pens, slippers, neck cushion, toothbrush, button-down shirts, socks, books, CDs, documents, coffee mug—were all scattered on the floor around her. Maybe that was why she'd dreamed of him.

Hinako curled into a ball and exhaled slowly. A crushing weight was pressing down on her chest.

Why? Why Minato of all people? What did he ever do to deserve this?

Hinako couldn't skip school forever, so she dragged herself to class. But she couldn't focus on the coursework; instead, she kept Minato's smartphone clutched in one hand at all times.

"Here, eat something." At the cafeteria, Jun bought her an egg sandwich.

Minato made egg sandwiches for us at Chigasaki Beach...and now I'll never get to taste them ever again.

"Have some coffee too." Ai handed her a paper cup full of steaming hot coffee.

It smelled wonderful. *Minato's coffee always tasted amazing...*

The memories, plus the kindness of the gesture, brought tears to Hinako's eyes.

"Hey, hey, hey!" Ai pulled out a handkerchief.

However, it was one Hinako had bought for Ai while on an aquarium date with Minato, and it was embroidered with porpoises all over. This brought to mind the porpoise hanging from the Bakeratta's rearview mirror. Finally, the dam burst, and Hinako broke down into sobs.

"Right, of course... Everything reminds you of him, doesn't it?" Jun said in a soothing voice as she pulled Hinako into her arms.

"I'm sorry..."

"Don't be."

"It's not your fault."

Once they'd heard about the accident, Jun and Ai started emailing Hinako several times a day to check in on her—short messages like "Good morning" and "Have you eaten something today?" Without those emails, Hinako probably would have faded away into an empty shell.

"You guys are so nice to me...even though you always used to tease me for being obsessed with him... You'd always call me a 'normie' and tell me to go to hell..."

"I'm sorry," said Ai.

"We were too harsh," said Jun.

She could feel Ai's body heat on her right side and Jun's on her left. *The living are so warm...*

"Whose is that?"

"Is that his phone?"

The two of them stared down at the phone Hinako was clutching.

"I don't know the passcode, so I can't unlock it," Hinako said. There was one question on her mind, one she hoped the phone might answer. "We always did everything together...but then, the morning after an all-nighter, he decided to go surfing all by himself...and I don't know why."

This mystery was the only thing keeping her going—that much was no exaggeration.

A tiny four-inch octopus floated in the water tank. Its brown body suddenly flared up bright yellow with blue rings all over.

That Saturday afternoon, Hinako had invited Youko to visit the aquarium.

"So *this* is a blue-ringed octopus, huh?" Youko peered at it curiously. Its blue rings looked like leopard spots.

"When's your birthday, Youko-chan?" Hinako asked, still holding Minato's phone.

"February 3rd."

Hinako entered *0203*–no dice.

"Meh, my stupid brother never bothered to remember my birthday."

"When's Marine Day?"

"It changes every year, remember?"

Oh. Right. "What's Disaster Prevention Day?"

"September 1st."

Hinako entered *0901*–that didn't work either. The phone refused to unlock. She looked around at the different species of jellyfish floating gracefully within their cylindrical tanks.

"It's none of our birthdays, and it's not the day of the fire, and it's not the day we first went surfing... None of these special dates are working."

Hinako had tried every number combination she could think of, and Youko was her last hope. But it was all in vain.

Just then, Youko stopped and glanced over her shoulder. "Why not ask Wasabi?"

"Who?"

"He came to your house with me to deliver the cardboard box. You remember him, right, Mukoumizu-san?"

"Oh, you mean Kawamura-san?"

Wasabi's first name was written in kanji on his business card, and she hadn't known it was pronounced Wasabi. *Why does everyone have such complicated names?*

"For the record, my name's actually Mukaimizu."

But Youko didn't seem to hear her. "Let's call him up and invite him to get coffee. He should be off work today."

"Oh, I recognize this place," Youko said.

They had arrived at Siren, the coffee shop. Siren was where Hinako and Youko had first met...except this was the Chiba branch, of course. As they walked in through the entrance, they caught sight of the brand-new dumbwaiter on the other side of the room.

"Apparently their main branch is in Chigasaki," Youko explained—probably secondhand knowledge from Minato—as they headed upstairs to the table where Wasabi was waiting. But Hinako already knew that, of course.

I'd like to run a café of my own someday, Minato had told her as he gazed out at the ocean. But this dream would never be fulfilled.

"The cool part is that they have a wide variety of brewing methods..."

"Whoa, no kidding. Anyway, I'll take a strawberry soda!"

Hinako remembered the disbelief on Minato's face after those words left her lips. Today, however, she ordered coffee like she was meant to... She could see her teary expression reflected on its surface.

Then, suddenly, she snapped to her senses. She had walked over to the dumbwaiter to fetch their order, and now she needed to take the tray back to their table.

"Sorry I took so—aaah!" In Hinako's haste, she accidentally dropped the tray.

"What's the matter with you?!" Youko shouted.

"Are you okay?!" Wasabi asked.

"I'm sorry!"

"Just stay right there! I'll go get a dishrag!" And with that, Wasabi raced downstairs.

Meanwhile, Hinako remembered the time at Chigasaki when she accidentally dropped the tray down the dumbwaiter shaft.

Minato, I haven't matured in the slightest since then... At the rate I'm going, I'll die an old woman before I ever find my true calling...

When Wasabi returned with some replacement drinks, once again, Hinako saw her weepy face reflected in the liquid.

"Will you knock it off? You're gonna ruin the coffee," Youko snapped at her.

"Sorry... I swear, I never used to be such a crybaby..."

"Yeah, well, grow the hell up!"

"Youko-chan!" Wasabi reprimanded her with a sharp look.

"Jeez, *excuse me* for being such a catty bitch."

"Nah, it's all right. You're fine just the way you are."

Youko evidently hadn't expected this response, because she looked at him in surprise, her cheeks flushed.

Unfortunately, Wasabi didn't know Minato's phone passcode either.

Why *had* he gone surfing by himself that morning? Perhaps the answer to Hinako's question would be locked away inside his phone forever...

Just then, Hinako realized exactly what song was playing over the store speakers.

"Oh, hey, I know this song. Senpai used to sing it all the time," Wasabi commented.

"Glittering sapphire as far as the eye can see..."

As Hinako sang along under her breath, bubbles sprang up in her water glass. *This isn't sparkling water, is it?*

"Bit by bit, you'll find that—"

Just then, out of nowhere, Minato's face appeared amid the bubbles.

"Huh?!" Hinako leaned in and stared closely. Was she so hung up on Minato that she was starting to hallucinate? She grabbed the glass, brought it right up to her eye level, and started blinking hard—but the hallucination didn't go away. Minato was right there, smiling and holding up a shaka.

"Minato?"

He was wearing a white shirt and jeans—not the most ideal attire for swimming but certainly in line with his usual style.

Meanwhile, Youko and Wasabi stared dubiously at Hinako.

"Uh...Hinako-san?" Wasabi asked hesitantly.

"I see Minato," Hinako murmured. If she told them that he was in her water glass, would they think she was crazy?

"What are you talking about? Seriously, what's wrong with you?!" Sure enough, Youko started shaking her by the shoulders.

"Ack!"

This knocked the glass from Hinako's hand. The water spilled all over the table, and Minato faded away.

"Minato..." Hinako stared dazedly at the mess.

"Listen here, you! My brother is *never* coming back! Now get it through your thick skull already!" Youko snarled.

These words pierced Hinako's heart like a thousand arrows. Youko was right, though. *How is it that a teenager somehow has it together more than I do?*

Hinako stared at the floor for a moment, then jumped to her feet and ran out of the café.

Whenever Hinako was at home, she always sat nestled between the boxes.

Once she regained her composure, she thought back over her experience at the café. Had it really been a hallucination? It felt so *real*...

Closing one eye, she held up her water bottle. But all she saw was clear water, sparkling in the sunlight streaming in through the window.

Come on out, Minato! She donned a grin and thrust out a shaka.

But he was nowhere to be seen.

The next morning, rain poured down in thick sheets as Hinako waited at the bus stop to catch a bus to school. Her mind wandered to a memory of her and Minato, sharing an umbrella as they walked down the street. At that time, Minato had sung their song: *"I see you there, looking at the water... Glittering sapphire as far as the eye can see..."*

Just like that, it was like Hinako had gone back in time. Before she knew it, she was singing along with him.

"Bit by bit, you'll find that its color will change... Kaleidoscopic majesty..."

As Hinako immersed herself in a happy delusion, she failed to notice the truck racing down the road in her direction, splashing up water from the puddles.

"But our lives won't always be sunshine... Now and then the rain will—huh?"

The next thing Hinako knew, something miraculous happened: the puddle water sprayed *over* her, creating a tunnel. And then—for the briefest of moments—she caught a glimpse of Minato in the water, flashing a shaka.

What's happening to me?

Back in reality, she could only stare into space in shock.

At college, Hinako spent the whole day ruminating on these

strange occurrences. She was in the restroom, staring at herself in the mirror as she dried her hands.

"Why does he keep appearing in the water...?"

Hinako put her hand back under the faucet, triggering the sensor to turn the water on. But how could she get Minato to show himself again?

"Is it the song...?"

Come to think of it, in both instances, she had been singing. Hesitantly, she began to sing again.

"I see you there, looking at the water... Wha?!"

Minato's smiling face rose up in the water pooling in the palm of Hinako's hand. Reflexively, she yanked her hand back; he splashed into the sink with the rest of the water, where he made shaka gestures with both hands.

Then, as Hinako watched in disbelief, he disappeared down the drain.

At this point, she couldn't keep it to herself anymore. She needed to tell someone...and the only people she could turn to were her two best friends.

"Hey, um..."

"What's up?" Jun replied.

"Is something wrong with me?" Hinako asked, staring at the ground as they walked. She had already decided not to comment on the crazy blue lipstick Jun was wearing.

"Physically or mentally?" Ai quipped, but Hinako ignored her.

"I mean...it's not normal to hallucinate, right?"

"You're not on an acid trip, are you?"

"God, I hope not. She's already a hot mess *without* adding hard drugs to the mix."

Uh, guys? If you want to dunk on me, could you at least sugar-coat it a little?

"I haven't done any drugs, but...I keep seeing Minato in the water." Hinako took a deep breath, then started to sing at the top of her lungs: "I see you there, looking at the water! Glittering—"

Then she dashed over to the campus pond and peered into the water. Sure enough, there he was!

"Minato!"

In response, he held up a shaka.

Then, when Jun and Ai ran over to join her, Hinako pointed down at the water. "See? He's doing a shaka!"

"Okay...maybe there *is* something wrong with you." Jun pulled Hinako into a tight hug.

"What if you went back to see your parents for a while? You should rest, Hinako," said Ai, placing a sympathetic hand on her shoulder.

Honestly, she didn't blame them for reacting the way they did.

It rained the next day too.

Hinako had forgotten her umbrella, so she raced across campus to the library, humming to herself as she went. She didn't seem to notice the raindrops dodging around her.

The library was newly built, with a big, fancy atrium and a skylight. On sunny days you could see the clear blue sky, but today the view was obscured by thick gray clouds. Raindrops splattered down on the glass in a polka dot pattern.

Still humming to herself, Hinako walked to the occult section and grabbed a book about earthbound spirits.

Let's see here... "Earthbound spirits are those who cannot accept or comprehend their own death. Thus, they remain trapped in one specific location." Is that what Minato is now? An earthbound spirit?

On a whim, Hinako looked up at the skylight. There, in the water droplets, was a tiny Minato. Then, right before her eyes, the raindrops gathered to spell out *HINAKO*, almost as if they had a mind of their own. She gasped, then turned to Jun and Ai and pointed at the ceiling.

"Look! Look at that! Look!"

But by the time they looked up, the water had trickled away.

Minato was everywhere. The café, the bus stop, the restroom sink, the pond, the library skylight...*everywhere.*

"It's Minato... I know it's him..."

Every time Hinako sang their song near a body of water, he was sure to appear.

Hinako crouched down on a bridge and flung a pebble into the low river below. With a splash, it sank into the water, leaving a ripple in its wake.

"So he's a ghost, and he can't move on to the afterlife? Is that why he only ever appears in water? Because he drowned?" Hinako rose to her feet and exhaled, then peered down into the water.

He's going to appear. I know it.

Just then, it occurred to her to pull her phone out prior to singing. She opened her camera app and switched it to video mode.

"Am I seriously trying to record ghost footage right now...?" she snarked under her breath. Then she began to sing. "I see you there, looking at the water... Glittering sapphire as far as the eye can see..."

Instantly, the river began to froth. And there, among the bubbles, was Minato.

"Ack!" *I forgot to hit Record!* Hastily, Hinako thrust her phone at the water. "Huh?! Gah!"

But her hand slipped, and the phone fell into the river.

Just then, however, the water rose up in a column towards her, carrying her phone on top, as if to return it to her. Timidly, Hinako reached out and took it...and the water column fell back into the river with a splash.

"I see you there, looking at the water..."

As Hinako sang, she hovered one foot in midair over the water—and the column rose up again to support her weight. She stepped onto it and found it surprisingly firm. Then she pulled her leg back. The column lowered.

Hinako stooped down and started singing louder. "Glittering sapphire as far as the eye can see!"

The water sprang up again. Surely it had to have a mind of its own—there was no other explanation. And so Hinako made up her mind. She walked in the opposite direction—then turned on her heel and sprinted toward the edge of the bridge, singing at the top of her lungs as she leapt into the air.

"I see you there, looking at the water! Glittering sapphire as far as the eye can see!"

Flailing her limbs, she plummeted downward. *Oh, God, please let me scrape by with some broken bones at worst!*

But the next thing she knew, the river rose up sharply to catch her. With a loud splash, she entered the water.

There, among the bubbles, was the same smile she had seen in her dreams.

"Minato!"

Hinako reached out to him, and he reached back. They couldn't touch. But Hinako didn't care. At last, she had reunited with her beloved.

As she popped her head out of the water, it slowly lowered down to her ankles. Meanwhile, Minato remained trapped just under the surface. Quietly, Hinako asked the only question that came to mind: "Why...?"

"I promised I'd always be there for you, didn't I?" he replied in a muffled voice at her feet. Then he threw up a shaka and grinned at her.

Ride your Wave

CHAPTER 4

Tube Riding

WAS HE A GHOST, a hallucination, or a miracle? Hinako didn't care. All that mattered was that Minato was back. Wearing a bath towel over her head, she spoke to the glass of water in her hand.

"Hi, Minato..."

"Hi, Hinako," Minato replied from inside. The water made his voice all wavery, but it was still the same loving voice she knew so well.

"This is so weird."

"I know."

Apparently his physical form changed size depending on the body of water he was summoned to, so right now he was the size of an action figure.

"What are you doing here? Did you...fail to pass on to the afterlife?"

"Maybe... I'm not sure," he replied, tilting his head in puzzlement.

"Was it because you had lingering regrets?"

"Or maybe my wish was granted." He glanced around. "I see you moved, huh?"

"Oh, uh...yeah..."

"You haven't been surfing?"

Hinako followed his gaze and found him looking at the orange surfboard leaning against the cardboard boxes.

"Looking at the ocean is...hard for me these days," she explained, looking away.

"I guess that's my fault... Sorry."

"No, don't be!" she replied, smiling and leaning in closer. "Anyway, forget all that! All I've ever wanted was to see you again... It feels like a dream come true!"

Night after night, she'd dreamed of Minato. Day after day, she'd bawled her eyes out, wishing her dream were real. But this time, it *was*.

"You'll show up in any body of water as long as I sing our song, right?"

"I don't really understand how it works, but...give me a call whenever you need me." Grinning, he threw up a shaka.

It's a divine miracle! Thank you, God, or Buddha, or whoever you are!

This was quite possibly the first time Hinako had smiled since Christmas, and she felt...stronger, somehow.

"Oh, uh! Youko-chan's doing well, by the way. And so is Wasabi-san."

"Yeah... I saw them briefly."

"Seems like they couldn't see you, though. Am I the only one who can?" She could just imagine how happy everyone would be if they could see him like she could.

"As long as you can see me, that's good enough for me."

"Well, okay... Oh, that reminds me!" She held up his phone in front of the glass. "Tell me your passcode!"

"What do you wanna look through my phone for?"

"I want to know why you went surfing without me."

"Well..." Minato fell silent and casually shifted his gaze to the floor. "I wanted to get some extra practice in so I could surprise you."

"Are you telling the truth...?"

Something felt fishy. Minato wasn't looking her in the eye when he spoke.

"Of course I am!" he shot back stubbornly, but this only made Hinako more suspicious. He put his hands on his hips. "I don't recall raising you to be the sort of girlfriend who would go through my phone without permission, young lady!"

"Well, maybe *you* should learn to share!"

Just then, Hinako felt the water dripping from her hair and realized she was still soaking wet from her impromptu river bath. Sure, it was almost March, but unlike Minato, she was in danger of getting sick if she didn't warm up.

"I'm gonna go take a bath, okay?" She rose from the box she was using as a chair. Then she glanced back over her shoulder. "You stay right there!" And with that, she walked into the bathroom.

Inside, she filled the tub with warm water, then lowered her body into it. Slowly, her clammy skin began to soften. Meanwhile, she was on cloud nine—Minato was in her living room!

"Does this mean...I'm living with Minato...?" The concept made Hinako bashful, and she pressed her hands to her cheeks. "First we move in together, and then we get married? I'm gonna be Hinageshi Hinako?" Giddy, she began to sing. "I see you there, looking at the water... Glittering sapphire as far as the eye can see..."

Just then, the bathwater began to bubble up loudly.

"Wha?!"

Between Hinako's legs, she could see Minato—

"AAAHH! Don't look, you pervert!" Covering her chest with her hands, she jumped out of the tub.

"I'm sorry! But you sang the song, so...!" He looked up at her from the bathwater, his expression perplexed.

Right. My mistake. Hinako sighed. "Sorry! You just startled me, that's all... Obviously I don't mind you seeing."

He wasn't some pervert—he was her boyfriend.

The next day, Hinako went to a large-scale supermarket and bought a clear portable water bottle. This way, she and Minato could be together at all times, even when she was on the go. She strapped it on diagonally across her chest and then set off on her bike, humming cheerfully to herself as she passed the fire station.

"Look, Minato! They're doing drills!"

She slowed to a stop and held up the water bottle so Minato could see. Come to think of it, this was the same spot where she'd been doused with hose water on the first day she moved back.

Minato gazed affectionately at his former coworkers as they trained hard.

"You really loved your job, huh?"

"Yeah."

If only Minato had never been a firefighter, maybe he wouldn't have died... No, there was no point in what-ifs. After all, his heroism was part of the reason she'd fallen for him in the first place.

Just then, she noticed one of the firefighters staring in their direction.

"What the? Wasabi-san?"

Hinako bowed her head in greeting, and Wasabi hastily bowed back.

It felt like all the color had returned to Hinako's world. She dragged Minato everywhere, like she was reliving their happy memories all over again.

First, she went to the Siren in Chigasaki, where she ate pancakes and ignored the weird looks she received from other customers as she talked to her water bottle.

Then she went to the pier where they had their first kiss. Minato gazed silently out at the sunset, and Hinako could only imagine how this trip was making him feel. But in place of words, she pressed her hand against the bottle.

Then she went to Chiba Port Tower. With the water bottle balanced on her head, she took another picture with the angel wing lights reflected in the windowpane, just like on Christmas Eve. Their heart-shaped padlock was still hanging there too.

Obviously things couldn't be *exactly* the same, but she could still see Minato's face, and hear his voice, and talk to him. And compared to the days she spent without him, she couldn't possibly ask for more. But...if Hinako was allowed to be a tiny bit greedy...she really missed being able to touch his body. That said, she knew it was beyond his control, seeing as he was a ghost and all.

On her way home, however, Hinako noticed other couples walking hand in hand...and she was struck with a brilliant idea. As soon as she got home, she connected a hose to the plastic inflatable porpoise and filled it up with water. Gleefully, she watched it fill up. And when she sang their song, sure enough, a full-sized Minato appeared inside.

"Yaaaay!"

She jumped into the porpoise's arms. Obviously, it felt nothing like his human body, but this way he felt a lot more real than the miniature water bottle version. Grabbing Minato by the fins, Hinako spun him around. *It's like he came back to life!*

They danced around the apartment until Minato fell to the floor. And when Hinako dove on top of him, the plug popped out, and he sprang a leak.

Minato had no regrets. If ever he had the chance to go back and do it all over again, he would make the same choice in a heartbeat. He was proud of himself for upholding his sworn duty as a firefighter. But he *did* have one lingering worry: Hinako.

He couldn't remember much of his death, but he remembered floating in darkness for a long time after the waves pulled him under. Perhaps that had been purgatory—the space between this world and the next.

Prior to his death, Hinako had never known Minato was a bad swimmer. How could he possibly tell her, when she was so convinced he was Superman? Chalk it up to his fragile male ego, but...her admiration had made him feel good about himself.

Then one day he heard her singing, and the next thing he knew, he was looking at her through the water. His vision was rounded, like he was looking through a fish-eye lens, and it felt like he'd turned into a porpoise...but in reality, he was probably some kind of ghost.

At first, Hinako was completely perplexed. No surprise there, of course; one minute she thought he was dead, and then he was in her water glass. But once she accepted that it was really him—she was either really open-minded, or optimistic, or she just didn't think too deeply, all perfectly valuable traits—she seemed to stop caring about any minor details whatsoever.

"Minato, let's go outside!"

It must have been surreal to watch a young woman lead a plastic porpoise full of water down the street. Minato did his best to keep up, walking along on his crescent-shaped tail fin.

The passersby all stared at Hinako as she passed, but she didn't pay them any mind.

"Which do you prefer, Minato?"

She had brought him to a plus-size men's clothing retailer. After propping him up in front of the mirror, she picked out a handful of shirts and made him try them on, one by one. And when he saw how happy it made her, he decided not to press the issue.

But time flies while you're having fun, as they say. And as they spent morning, noon, and night together, the seasons changed... and the dogwood trees began to bloom.

One night, at Hinako's request, they paid a visit to a newly built shopping mall.

"Minato!"

She was skipping along, leading him by the hand like usual, when she suddenly looked over her shoulder at him. With each movement, her white dress fluttered like the wings of a little white butterfly. She was adorable.

"I wanna get some gelato. Ooh, and bubble tea!"

While Hinako was distracted talking to Minato, a man popped out of a store just ahead of them, and the two nearly crashed into each other.

"Gah!"

The guy managed to dodge away in the nick of time, but Hinako fell to the floor.

"Ow ow ow..."

"You scared me! You okay?" the man asked her. In his hemp jacket, he gave off something of a surfer vibe.

"I'm so sorry about that!"

The guy offered her a hand, and Hinako took it, rising to her feet once more. Minato had offered her his fin too, but she seemingly hadn't noticed.

"Where are you from?" the guy asked, casually placing a hand on her back.

Hey! Don't touch my girlfriend like she's yours! But alas, the porpoise couldn't speak.

"Um...Chiba..."

"Oh, so you're a local. Anyway, I see you've got a big boy here with you..."

He was a smooth talker, and Minato could tell he was totally a ladies' man. Hinako seemed a little flushed in the cheeks. Was he her type?

Feeling like a third wheel, Minato stared down at his hand— and gasped. It was...fading...? Startled, he looked down at his feet. His toes were fading too.

The time he spent with Hinako was so much fun, he had somehow forgotten he was a ghost... No, that wasn't quite right. They had both been through so much pain, he couldn't help but want to avert his eyes from the truth for a tiny bit longer.

Somewhere, deep down...he knew he wouldn't be able to stay with her forever.

That evening, the two of them went back to the local beach.

"Is something wrong?" Hinako asked, leaning in and tilting her head. Clearly his worry showed on his face.

"Oh, it's just... I wish I could hold your hand. Or help you up, like that other guy did. But I can't."

"Wait a minute... Don't tell me you're *jealous*!" she teased.

Minato scowled. "I'm not."

"I'm not going to cheat on you, Minato. You're the only one for me."

"I told you, I'm not jealous!" he shouted, and Hinako flinched back. Come to think of it, this was the first time he'd ever raised his voice at her.

"We're finally having our first fight, huh? C'mon, cheer up," she continued playfully as she gave the inflatable porpoise a little smooch. And as she giggled bashfully, he found her more adorable than ever.

He wanted nothing more than to hold her tightly in his arms... but of all the wishes in all the world, that one could never come true.

"Gimme one more."

"Oh ho! Greedy, are we?" Hinako feigned surprise, then gleefully buried her face in the plastic. "*Mmmmmwah!* Now can you forgive me?"

"No."

"Aww, c'moooon!" she wailed dramatically.

"Can I ask you for another favor?"

"What is it this time?"

Her expression was one of amusement, but he stared back intently.

"Take me out on the water."

At this, her face fell.

"I want to see you surf one last time."

But Minato's return hadn't pushed Hinako forward. Unbeknownst to him, she had only regressed.

The sea was dotted with surfers awaiting the arrival of the next wave. Dressed in her wetsuit, Hinako stared out at them from the shore, surfboard in one hand, Minato's porpoise fin in the other.

One of the surfers on the outer side caught a wave. His techniques were downright captivating. After a display like that, anyone with a board would be itching to get out on the water themselves. Just then, another surfer with a twin-fin board did a takeoff in the first surfer's direction.

In surfing, there was a general rule: one surfer per wave. To snake on someone else's wave was a taboo of the highest order, not to mention extremely dangerous. Sure enough, the two surfers nearly collided, and one of them got knocked off his board into the water.

Hinako gasped, and all the blood drained from her face. Maybe the wipeout reminded her of the accident... Either way, she was clearly in no condition to surf, so Minato decided they should rest on a nearby bench instead.

"I'm sorry," she muttered, slumping her shoulders.

"If anyone should apologize, it's me. I should have taken your feelings into account before I made that stupid request," Minato replied as he sat beside her, gazing at her with concern.

"When I was little, I used to live around here..." she began slowly. "Back then, surfing came second nature to me. But right now I don't even know how to paddle, literally *or* figuratively..." She leaned forward and buried her face in her hands.

When Minato first saw Hinako surfing from the roof of the fire station, he had half-wondered if the water was supporting her of its own free will, like it had a mind of its own. She used to be confident and fearless. But now she was utterly defeated.

Don't give up.

Minato started to reach out to her...but his hand balled into a fist. With his stubby little porpoise fins, he couldn't even put an arm around her shoulders.

"If you think about it, the ocean is pretty powerful," he said. "Even the smallest waves are still strong enough to travel all the way to the shore. I know it might be a little overwhelming for you right now, but these waves will pass—me included. You've just gotta get out there and wait for the next one."

Hinako looked up sharply. "Don't talk about yourself like that! All I need is you! I'll stay with you my whole life!"

You can't, Hinako. You have to move on...before I run out of time. Minato said, "I'll support you until you can ride the waves on your own again. I love you, and I want you to succeed."

He tossed up a shaka and gave it a shake. But Hinako frowned sadly and didn't return the gesture.

Minato floated inside a column of water rising up from Hinako's bathtub all the way to the ceiling. She approached, wearing a yellow bikini. Then she placed both hands on the wall of water and slowly stepped in.

He was the one who had initially suggested this. Sure, maybe they couldn't ride the waves together, but they could still swim together.

In the water, nothing could keep them apart. They drew close as if magnetized to each other...but the moment they made contact, he burst into bubbles and reformed.

Together, they swam around for as long as Hinako could hold her breath.

He wanted to kiss her. To touch her. Impassioned, he leaned against her lips, but swiftly burst into bubbles once more. In bubble form, he drifted along her arms, legs, torso...

"When I'm in the water, it feels like I'm wrapped up in your arms." Hinako closed her eyes and relaxed like she was finally at peace.

The cicadas are so whiny this year, Wasabi thought to himself as he wiped the sweat from his brow with the back of his hand. Then he opened the door and walked into Siren.

"Welcome, welcome!" called Youko, dressed in her employee uniform and carrying an empty tray under her arm. Then she looked over her shoulder, and when she saw who it was, her face lit up. "What the heck? What are you doing here?"

"Mom told me you started working here part-time, and... I wanted to talk to you about something."

"Hey, boss! I'm going on break!"

Are you allowed to decide that for yourself? he wondered, mildly perplexed. But thankfully, the manager seemed like a pretty chill guy. He nodded his assent with a smile.

"Here, drink up," said Youko as she brought Wasabi the daily special. Together, they sat down at a table by the windows. "So what brings you all the way here?"

For a moment he debated how to broach the subject, but then she beat him to the punch. "Relax, Wasabi. You're fine just the way you are."

"Uh, Youko-chan...?"

"Oniichan said as much himself, right? Just cheer up."

Evidently she had jumped to the wrong conclusion.

"Actually, no, uh, this isn't about my job."

"It's not?"

"No. It's about...Hinako-san."

The instant her name left his lips, Youko's mood took a nose-dive. "Oh, I *see*," she spat, propping her chin on her elbow in a blatant display of disinterest.

"She's acting weird lately," he continued.

"So what? She's always been weird."

"She's been talking to her water bottle. And walking around town with Senpai's inflatable porpoise. It's like...like she thinks the water *is* him."

Wasabi had first noticed this during hose drills the other day, when he heard Hinako say to her water bottle: *Look, Minato! They're doing drills!* Then, a few days later, he spotted her on the street, walking hand in hand with Minato's inflatable porpoise in a Hawaiian shirt. He didn't know if she was mentally unbalanced or what, but something was clearly wrong... So from that day forward, he'd spent each weekend checking in on her.

One time, Hinako and the porpoise went rowing in the pond at the park—Hinako did all the rowing herself. Worse, she talked to the thing like it was alive. Definitely not something a sane person would do! Not only that, she even took it onto the train with her, complete with a packed lunch, fully ignoring all the weird looks she got. (Then, when she started playing card games with it, they all averted their eyes.)

"You've been *stalking her*?!" Youko scoffed, scandalized. But that was the furthest thing from Wasabi's intention.

"I was just...worried..."

"Why?"

"Good question... I mean, Senpai was always watching her from the station roof, so I started watching her too, and...the next thing I knew, I... But she was his girlfriend, so..."

Youko listened to this awkward confession with her lips curled in disgust.

"Er, sorry, I'm going off-topic! The point is, uh, I'm worried about her current condition... Really, really worried..."

"How stupid are you?"

"Huh?!"

"If you're so worried about her, then tell *her*! To her *face*! You're in love with her, right? So why are you telling *me*?!"

Wasabi couldn't argue with this. It was an extremely good point.

"But just so you know, dating is for *squares*!" She slammed her hands on the table and jumped to her feet. "Hey, boss! My break's over!"

And with that, she stormed off...leaving Wasabi alone at the table, hanging his head.

"Nngh!"

Hinako grunted as she hoisted a bucket of poppy anemones with both hands. The soil was waterlogged, which made it extra heavy, and she staggered bowlegged to the door. It was almost time to close up shop, so her task was to bring all the products back in for the night.

She set the bucket down in the front of the door and opened it. Then, using her head to keep the door ajar, she bent down to grab the bucket again. This was a skill she had picked up over the past ten months of working at the florist's. But today the buckets were heavier than usual, and she was really struggling.

Just then, a hand reached out from behind her and opened the door for her.

"Whoa!"

As Hinako lost her balance, water splashed up out of the bucket and onto her apron.

"Sorry!" It was Wasabi. He hastily pulled a towel out of his bag and handed it to her. "Here! I, uh, was meaning to return this to you."

Wait, what the? It was the very same towel she'd given that firefighter on her first day back... Then it finally clicked.

"That was *you*?!" Hinako exclaimed. *You were the guy who sprayed me with the fire hose?!*

"You only *just now* put that together...?" Wasabi slumped his shoulders.

"I'm sorry! Anyway, no need. It was just a splash," she shrugged. "So, are you here to buy some flowers?"

"Oh, uh, yeah!"

If the customer was male, there was a 99 percent chance the flowers were a gift for a woman. But while most men chose flowers in red or pink, Wasabi was an exception.

"I hope the recipient likes their flowers," she told him as she handed him the finished bouquet. But for some reason, he started to panic.

"Oh, uh! Well, she really loves the ocean, so I figured I'd do blue and white, but...maybe that's kinda dorky..."

"That's not dorky at all! It's a wonderful idea."

"Oh, thank goodness!"

Blue poppies and white roses—both among Hinako's favorites.

"I notice you don't have your friends with you today."

"Huh?"

"You know, that water bottle you've been carrying around?"

Hinako's heart skipped a beat. How did Wasabi know? She averted her gaze. "Well, I'm on the clock, so..."

"Or that giant inflatable porpoise?"

Now *that* made her panic. "What?! How do you know about that?!"

"Well, I've seen you around...at the station, on the street... I wanted to say hi, but it was too awkward because...I mean, you were talking to your water bottle like it was Senpai!" Wasabi took a step closer as he spoke.

"I'm sorry! I was just talking to myself, that's all!"

"But still...!"

"Uhh, y-you should take your flowers and get going! Before they wilt!"

Changing the subject, Hinako pushed the bouquet into his arms...but for some reason, he turned around and offered them back to her.

"Actually, uh...these are for you."

"What?! But you said she loves the ocean, and I—"

"I've always had feelings for you, deep down!" Wasabi interrupted, blushing. "Don't you think maybe I could be good for you too?! Couldn't I make you happy?! I love you, and I want you to be happy!"

Wasabi thrust the flowers firmly in her face. But it was all so sudden—Hinako couldn't think straight.

"I, uh...I mean...I...I...I'm sorry!"

And with that, Hinako dashed into the staff bathroom and shut the door.

Wasabi's declaration of love had been completely out of left field. Panicking, Hinako started singing into the toilet.

"I see you there, looking at the water!"

The toilet water bubbled, and Minato quickly appeared. "What's up, Hinako?"

"It's Wasabi-san... He...!"

"He what?!" Minato turned white as a sheet. Perhaps his first thought was that Wasabi had been injured in the line of duty.

"He just told me he has feelings for me!" Hinako told him point-blank.

Minato fell silent for a moment and then looked up at her. "Well, how do you feel about it?"

"Me?! I'm only interested in *you*!"

"But I'm *dead*, Hinako. I can't hold your hand, or hug you, or kiss you..."

To be fair, yes, she missed doing all that. Especially since she could remember how nice it felt. But...

"He's a good guy, you know."

"Minato..."

"Trust me, I can tell. He's kindhearted, and sincere, and..."

I can't believe this. Are you seriously telling me to get with him?! Hinako stared. "Are you listening to yourself right now?! I told you, I'm happy with the way things are now! I can see you whenever I want! Sure, maybe we can't hug or hold hands, but at least you're always around! That's all I need!"

"Hinako, calm down! Your coworker's looking at you funny!"

"Huh?!"

Hinako looked over at the door, and sure enough, one of the other employees was peering at her through the crack. *Crap,*

I forgot to lock it! She hastily jumped to her feet and remedied her mistake.

"Sorry, I wasn't thinking…"

"Listen to me, Hinako," Minato said quietly. "These new waves are going to keep coming at you, one after another. Sure, some of them will be too small to ride, but if you keep hiding in the water, you'll never move forward."

Minato's words weighed heavily on her shoulders.

But by the time Hinako left the bathroom, Wasabi was nowhere to be found…and in his place, the bouquet was lying forgotten on the table.

Hinako dashed out of the flower shop in pursuit of Wasabi.

To be clear, she wasn't going to date him just because Minato encouraged her to, like some kind of new coffee blend he wanted her to try. But regardless, Wasabi deserved an apology for the awful way she'd gone about shooting him down.

When Hinako reached the main street intersection, she spotted him standing on the bridge, looking out over the river. Judging from the sigh he heaved, he was devastated.

I need to do this the right way.

"Wasa—"

But just then, there was an earsplitting screech, followed by the sound of a hard impact. Near the intersection, a semi-truck had crashed into a small passenger car, which was now on fire.

As Hinako froze in fear, Wasabi ran over to her. "Hinako-san!"

The instant he shielded her, the passenger car exploded.

A few other cars rolled to a stop, and the drivers hopped out.

"Somebody call 119!"

"There's been an accident!"

The local residents flooded out onto the sidewalk, and it turned into a spectacle.

"The driver hasn't made it out of the passenger car," Hinako whispered. Reflexively, she took a step forward. But Wasabi stopped her.

"It's too late. You can't save them."

"But they're still in there!"

Hinako pushed forward, but Wasabi used his full force to stop her. "It's not safe!"

"If Minato was here, he would try to save them!" Trapped in Wasabi's arms, Hinako started singing at the top of her lungs. "I see you there, looking at the water! Glittering sapphire as far as the eye can see!"

"Hinako-san!"

"Bit by bit, you'll find that its color will change!"

Please, Minato! Please save the driver!

Bubbles rose from the depths of the river, and the water rose up in a high column that crashed into the burning car. With a loud sizzle, the fire was extinguished, and steam rose up in its place.

Moments later, the fire department arrived on the scene; Minato watched them work from inside the rising steam cloud. The passenger car was completely totaled, and when the rescue workers pulled the driver's body from the wreckage and loaded him onto a stretcher, it was clear he was already gone. Sadly, he had died instantly upon impact.

Human beings were fragile creatures that could lose their lives in an instant—that much Minato knew from firsthand experience. That was what made life so precious.

But just then, a light shone down from the heavens onto the stretcher, and the soul of the victim rose up into the air, as if summoned. Then, as Minato watched this unfold, a light suddenly shone down onto him as well. He felt a tremendous power pulling him upward.

No! Don't take me! Please! Struggling, he reached out to Hinako and Wasabi below.

"Minato?!" Hinako shrieked.

"What's wrong?!" Wasabi asked her.

"It's Minato! I can't hear his voice!"

Hinako! Minato reached out to her desperately, but to no avail. The light was swallowing him up.

"They're taking him away! *Minato!*" Hinako screamed, half-delirious, as Wasabi did his best to hold and soothe her.

"Hinako-san!"

"He'll vanish!"

"Hinako-san, snap out of it!" Wasabi shook her by the shoulders. "I don't mean to hurt you, but Senpai is gone, and there's no such thing as ghosts!"

"You're WRONG!" Hinako shoved his hands away. "Maybe *you* can't see him, but he's there! In the water! He appears every time I sing—I see him! He's real, and he's there! He's always there!"

"I admit, from the way he loved you, I wouldn't be surprised if he fought tooth and nail to claw his way back to you." Wasabi started to reach out to her, but then thought better of it and drew his hand back. "But I know for a fact he wouldn't want to see you like this!"

Hinako stared back wordlessly. Her chest ached as her mind replayed the last words Minato had spoken to her:

If you keep hiding in the water, you'll never move forward.

"A long time ago, Senpai told me that you were his hero. Remember how you used to go out and surf the waves all by yourself? You were so strong. What happened to you?"

"I get it, okay? I get it already!" Hinako turned and took off running down the street. *Screw this.*

"If you keep acting like this, he'll never be able to pass on!"

I know, I know, I KNOW!

"Hinako-san!"

Wasabi's voice was all that chased after her.

The front door flew open, and Hinako dashed into her apartment.

"Minato!"

She flipped on the lights and spotted the inflatable porpoise sagging lifelessly on the floor. Hastily, she affixed one end of her hose to the valve and the other end to the bathroom faucet. Slowly but surely, the porpoise straightened back up again.

"I see you there, looking at the water! Glittering sapphire as far as the eye can see!"

Inside, Minato faintly reappeared. "Hina...ko...?"

"I'm so sorry, Minato! I shouldn't have called for you all those times! Has it been too much for you?"

It probably took a lot of energy to manifest back in the real world. Maybe that was why he was starting to fade away.

"What do I do...? I don't want you to disappear... I'm so sorry...!" Her pained sobs echoed through the empty apartment.

The river, the ocean... There was water everywhere she looked, and yet...

"I see you—"

Hinako started to sing but quickly stopped herself. As badly as she wanted to see Minato and talk to him, she knew the next time she summoned him might very well be the last—and the mere thought was *unbearable*. She'd already been through enough heartbreak for one lifetime; the last thing she wanted was to go back to the days she spent living in a fog.

On her bike, she pedaled to Siren.

"Welc—" Youko took one look at Hinako and switched off her customer-service smile.

"Have a seat wherever you like," she muttered, gesturing around at the tables with a snotty attitude unfitting of a waitress.

Once Hinako was seated, Youko brought over a menu and a glass of ice water and then practically slammed them down on the table.

"At our café, we specialize in offering a wide variety of brewing methods for our coffee," she explained, reciting her lines in a deadpan voice as she held up a visual aid. "Personally, I recommend drip coffee. But whatever you decide, make sure it isn't the strawberry soda."

"I'm impressed, Youko-chan!"

She scowled. "Did you come here to mock me?"

"Of course not!" Hinako replied hastily. "I just heard you started working here—"

"From who? Wasabi?" Youko asked quickly.

"Uhh, yeah...?"

"Did he say anything else?"

"Huh? Er... N-not really...?" she lied.

But Youko saw straight through her. "God, I wish I was a blue-ringed octopus! I'd bite his freaking face off!"

"Huh?"

"Nothing! Forget it!" For some reason, Youko's face looked a little flushed...or was Hinako seeing things?

"So what made you decide to get a job here?"

"Well, I've decided I want to run my own café someday."

"What...?"

"My brother's biggest dream was to open a café, and I'm going to make it happen."

She's doing it for him? Hinako couldn't believe it.

"So I figure I'll work here part-time while I get my diploma. Do you know why coffee grinds expand during drip brewing? It's because they release carbon dioxide. These gases are initially formed during the roasting process. Then, once the beans are ground up, the CO_2 starts to escape at a faster rate until eventually it goes stale. So the more it puffs up, the fresher it is."

The way Youko smugly parroted this information, she sounded exactly like her big brother.

"Once I graduate from high school, I'm gonna go and do some training at the main branch in Chigasaki. The owners are so old, they might kick the bucket any day now." In contrast to Youko's caustic phrasing, her eyes shone with warmth.

"You amaze me, Youko-chan," Hinako said after a moment. It was the honest truth.

Youko had spotted her next wave up ahead, and now she was getting ready to swim for it. By comparison, Hinako was a total coward. She couldn't even plan for *tomorrow*, let alone the rest of her life. Her biggest fear was losing Minato's ghost.

Later, on her way home, Hinako passed behind the fire station. The firefighters were decked out in their full gear, doing rope drills. On a whim, she stopped her bike and watched them.

Wow... That's incredible. They're so high up, and the rope is so thin, but they make it look so easy!

"Go, go, go, go!"

"Wasabi! Hang in there!"

Gritting his teeth, Wasabi made his way across the rope bridge as the other firefighters cheered him on. And in that moment, he looked downright unstoppable.

The Hinageshi residence was right on the water, with only the road separating it from the beach. In the empty lot next door, Minato's Bakeratta sat forgotten. This building had housed three generations of Hinageshis thus far, and with its wooden shingle roof, weathered supports, and faded brown chest of drawers in the living room, Hinako could feel all the history behind it.

Following the traditional ritual, she placed a stick of incense on Minato's memorial altar, knelt before his portrait, and pressed her hands together in prayer. Then she turned and bowed deeply to Youko, who was standing behind Hinako with a morose expression on her face.

"Why even bother paying your respects after all this time?"

"I'm sorry I didn't come by sooner. I had a hard time accepting he was gone."

Hinako had been present for the start of Minato's funeral but ultimately ran out before they even lit the incense. She couldn't bear the thought of having to look at his corpse.

"Where are your parents?" Hinako asked, glancing around.

"At work," Youko replied. "They've only just recovered, so they can't really handle reminiscing about my brother right now."

Ah. Now Hinako understood why, when she requested a visit, Youko had insisted it take place on a weekday afternoon. "Sorry for making things complicated."

"They've left his room the way it was... You wanted to see it, right?" Youko muttered, her face turned away.

"Right."

For as blunt as she was, Youko was a sensitive and empathetic girl, and Hinako treasured her like a sister...but if she admitted this out loud, Youko would probably just roll her eyes, so Hinako kept it to herself.

As Youko opened the door to Minato's room, Hinako's eyes widened. The whole room was filled with *books, books, books* from floor to ceiling—with a tiny space allocated for some workout equipment.

"Everyone always thought my brother was born perfect, but the truth is, he worked his ass off. He just never let it show."

The bookshelves were packed tight with firefighting workbooks, academic textbooks in every subject, books about coffee, books about running a café, cookbooks, and recipe binders labeled by type of cuisine.

"Growing up, our parents were always busy with work, so Oniichan had to make dinner for us. And in the beginning, the stuff he made was almost inedible."

Youko recalled the story of Minato, wearing an apron that was too big for him, struggling to maneuver a frying pan full of burnt fried rice.

"Then he read a bunch of cookbooks and watched some cooking shows, and the next thing I knew, he was suddenly good at it."

At his young age, he somehow mastered the wok and started serving restaurant-quality fried rice at the dinner table. But he always ate his food in silence, even if it was burnt black.

"And even after he was hired as a firefighter, he kept studying. His pet phrase was 'If I don't keep swimming, I'll sink like a rock.' I don't know how he did it."

Youko smiled and shook her head.

"After he died, a whole bunch of people came to pay their respects. And every one of them told us that he'd helped them in some way."

Dozens of people had knelt before Minato's altar—male and female, young and old. The Hinageshi family could scarcely believe it. There was an old lady who said Minato helped her after she threw her back out in the middle of the street...a teenage boy whose wallet he had recovered...a mother-and-child pair who he had reunited...a middle-aged man whose tire he helped change...a young corner store cashier who he had shielded after a customer started making a scene...a middle-aged woman whose wheelchair he pushed up a hill... Minato had impacted all of their lives, and his memory was alive inside each and every one of them. This had been the family's sole silver lining in the midst of their grief.

"My brother's goal was always to help people, and he first got the idea from a near-death experience he had when he was younger. See, the girl who saved him was even younger than he was. That was what inspired him to try to make a difference in the world." As she spoke, Youko stepped into the room. "He would always say 'A hero saved my life, so now it's *my* turn to be the hero.' That's why he dedicated his life to rescue work."

Youko pulled an album from one of the shelves, flipped halfway through it, and held it up for Hinako to see. "He said that experience changed his life and gave him a purpose."

Inside were photos of the beach. One featured a young Minato and Youko wearing swim rings and facing away from the camera. He must have been in third or fourth grade in this picture. On the seat of his teal swim trunks was the silhouette of a sea turtle...

Hinako gasped in shock as her eyes widened. Meanwhile, a flashback rose up in her mind. Could it be...? Was Minato...*him*?

She dashed out of the room.

"What's gotten into you this time...?" Holding the album, Youko sighed and watched Hinako go.

CHAPTER 5

Roller Coaster

"**Y**OU ONLY JUST GOT HERE! What are you looking for?" asked Hinako's mother as she carried in some barley tea and watermelon. Not only had her daughter turned up with no advance notice, now she was practically tearing through the old family albums.

"Didn't I rescue a boy from the ocean when I was a kid?!"

"Oh, that! You really made headlines back then. Just a moment."

Mrs. Mukaimizu headed back into the kitchen and used a chair to reach one of the cupboards. From there, she produced an alligator-print cylindrical tube and popped off the lid. The momentum sent a scrap of paper fluttering out to the floor. It was an old newspaper clipping titled "Certificate of Heroism," and it featured a photograph of young Hinako holding up her certificate with one hand and a shaka with the other.

"You were a certified hero!" Mrs. Mukaimizu laughed.

The incident made headlines because of their age difference—a first-grade girl rescuing a fourth-grade boy.

Fourteen-year-old memories revived in Hinako's mind one after another. At the time, she remembered hearing a popular song playing from someone's boom box...

I see you there, looking at the water
Glittering sapphire as far as the eye can see
Bit by bit, you'll find that its color will change
Kaleidoscopic majesty...

School was out for the summer, and Hinako's father had brought her to Kujukuri Beach during the height of surfing season. She had only recently learned how to surf, but she was a natural, and now she was *obsessed* with it. After all, she was such a "water child," she learned how to swim before she properly learned how to walk.

Riding on the porpoise surfboard her parents had bought for her, Hinako swam out among the grown-ups and waited for a wave to come. In the distance, she could see a boy with one arm around a swim ring, doggy-paddling in the direction of the shore. He was trying his best to practice, but he wasn't doing too well.

Hinako glanced at the beach—and when she looked back, the boy was gone. Only the swim ring remained floating on the surface.

He's drowning!

Hinako reacted on instinct, paddling desperately over to the swim ring. She could see bubbles faintly rising to the surface, so she took a deep breath and plunged underwater. There, she saw the boy from earlier slowly sinking to the bottom of the ocean— so she hauled him back up to the surface.

Gasping for breath, she swam around to the opposite side of her surfboard and pulled the boy's larger, unconscious body onto it.

"Nnnngh!"

Hinako's board flipped over, and the boy slid onto it face-down. Hinako didn't know it at the time, but this was actually the correct rescue method for women and children to perform. Breathing hard, she knelt on the tail of her board and started paddling toward the shore.

Her only thought: *I have to save him.*

"That was incredible!"

"You rock, little girl!"

Partway through, some grown-up surfers took over for her. A bunch of lifeguards were waiting on the beach when they arrived; someone had the quick thinking to wave them over. They started CPR right away.

The boy's face was as pale as a corpse, and he showed no signs of stirring. Standing beside her father, Hinako held her surfboard and prayed desperately: *Please, don't die!*

"When the ambulance gets here, direct them over!"

Just then—the boy started coughing. The crowd cheered, and the lifeguards rolled him onto his side so he could get all the water out.

Hinako could remember the intense relief she felt knowing the boy was alive, and the feeling of her father's hand ruffling her hair. "You did good, sweetheart."

Then one of the lifeguards spoke to the boy.

"You see that little girl? She saved your life. She's your hero."

Hinako thought back to her conversation with Youko:

—*That's why he dedicated his life to rescue work.*

And on Christmas Eve, Minato had told her about what inspired him to become a firefighter:

—*When I was a kid, I almost drowned out in the ocean. But someone saved me. I remember it all like it was yesterday... I wanted to work in a field where I could help people.*

And that song too:

—*It got featured in a movie recently, so they're playing it on the radio again.*

Had Minato intentionally played that song for her as a sort of hint?

All along, he'd known she was the same girl who saved his life as a child.

When Hinako was ferrying him to shore, all she could see were two things: the porpoise decal on her board and the sea turtle on his trunks. The same two animals hanging from the Bakeratta's rearview mirror...

On the train platform, Hinako sat on the bench. After the way she'd dashed out of her parents' house, even her own mother had to think she was a nutcase. But she needed some alone time in order to test something.

Clutched in her hands were two objects: the newspaper clipping and Minato's smartphone. According to Youko, his near-death experience "changed his life and gave him a purpose." Date: August 8th, 2006.

She punched in *8806*.

"Oh..."

At last, Minato's phone unlocked.

She opened his LINE app. At the very top was her own name—she was the last person he had messaged before his death. She tapped the conversation and found an unfinished message typed into the chat bar:

"Hinako! I rode those post-snow waves and pulled off an air reverse! You said it'll make my wish come true, right? So I wished for you to learn how to ride your own wave...and for me to always, always, always be by your side."

That was where the message ended—and it was exactly the answer Hinako was looking for. That morning, Minato had gone surfing with her in mind.

Her hand trembled as it clutched his phone.

He did it all for a girl as hopeless as me.

A hot lump rose in her throat.

Minato, why do you always have to be so sweet? Why do you always coddle me?

Hinako tilted her head up, fighting the tears that threatened to spill out.

Tell me, Minato... How can I ever repay you for the love you've given me?

The next day, Hinako paid a visit to the campus recreation center. As it turned out, there were a lot of different sports teams and liberal arts clubs at her college. Maybe she would have noticed sooner if she weren't always so hyper-focused on surfing.

"Interested in lifeguard training?"

As she looked over the posters and photos on the bulletin board, it just so happened that she was called out to by the captain of the very club she was looking to visit: the Lifeguard Club.

"Our club attracts people from all walks of life, from seasoned surfers to folks who can't swim. And while we'd love it if everyone could learn how to rescue people from the water, our main focus is on accident prevention," the captain explained as he led Hinako to their clubroom. "For some people, their goal is just to get certified. Others compete in lifeguarding events."

He showed her the storage room where they kept their canoes and surfboards. Then he brought her into the clubroom and showed her their extensive collection of life vests, stretchers, and other lifesaving equipment. They were so well equipped, they seemed less like a casual college club and more like a full-scale organization.

"The guy-to-girl ratio is about 60-40. In the summer we go on club trips to patrol the beach, and we take part in those competitions I mentioned too."

The reason Minato had never sent his last message was probably because he stopped to rescue that drowning man before hitting Send...

On the train home from her parents' place, Hinako had done a Google search for "jobs that help people." A lot of results had popped up: lawyer, teacher, certified caregiver, police officer, social worker, firefighter...and lifeguard.

According to the internet, she would need to study a lot of different subjects to get her certification: lifeguarding, beach safety, surf lifesaving, emergency first aid, CPR, and more. And since studying wasn't her favorite thing in the world, this was quite possibly a massive hurdle to overcome. But hey—even Minato had been able to overcome his poor swimming skills in order to be a firefighter, right?

Like a sea turtle, I'll just have to chase after him...right into the ocean.

Wasabi jogged along the beachside road. With each breath, sweat dripped down his body. If only it were that easy to get the heartbreak out of his system, but alas. As worried as he was, Hinako had rejected his help...

"Hey, loser!" a cheerful voice called. He looked up to find Youko waving at him up ahead, wearing a short-sleeved hoodie and shorts. "You train on your days off too?"

She poured some beans into a coffee grinder and started cranking the handle. This was Minato's coffee-making equipment, which Youko had chosen to inherit as a memento. She used his drip-brewing method to make coffee for the two of them.

Minato had always been such a coffee geek. Wasabi must have heard him ramble about beans and brewing and all that nonsense a dozen times.

"I check the fire hydrants as often as I can, because the city likes to move them around a lot, and the next thing I knew, it just sorta... turned into a jogging routine. Not that it's even my job to check 'em."

"Oniichan used to patrol the city too. 'An ounce of prevention is worth a pound of cure,' as he always put it."

"Man, he was one hell of a guy, wasn't he? I'll never be like him, no matter how hard I try."

"Of course not."

"Right..." Wasabi let out a dry laugh. *I'll never win Hinako-san's love. She would sooner choose a water spirit over me.*

Honestly, the battle for her heart had been settled during the fire at her apartment complex, when Wasabi arrived at the rooftop just in time to see Minato carry her away.

"What made you decide to be a firefighter, Wasabi?" Youko asked.

"Isn't it obvious? Because fire trucks are badass! I always wanted to learn how to drive one, y'know?"

"That's not the first reason that comes to my mind, but all right." Laughing, she handed him his coffee.

"Thanks."

"Sugar's in here." Youko gestured to a plastic container with raw sugar inside.

"Maybe I should've thought harder before committing my whole life to this career. Want some?" After adding sugar to his own drink, Wasabi added some to Youko's too.

"Ah...!"

"I always considered myself athletic, but man, this job really takes a physical toll on you..." This was something Wasabi struggled with all through firefighting academy, and it hadn't improved since he was formally hired. Minato had always been his one source of encouragement at work. Without him, Wasabi probably would have quit the force a long time ago.

"No matter how much effort I put in, I'll never be like Senpai was. I can't save lives... I'm just not cut out to be a firefighter." Wasabi took a sip of his coffee and frowned. "Not strong enough."

"You can say that again," Youko replied with a scowl.

Oh. Maybe I should've put more sugar in hers. Wasabi winced. "Sorry... I'm not a coffee expert like Senpai was."

"Will you shut up about my stupid brother?! You don't *have* to be like him! You can just be *yourself*!"

Wasabi hadn't expected Youko to reassure him like this, so he floundered for a moment. "I can't believe it... You actually said something nice for a change..."

"Don't you *get it*, you idiot?! I'm just repeating your own words right back at you!"

"Huh?"

"Remember that time when my mom was comparing me to my brother? You stood up for me and said I was fine just the way I was."

Wasabi vaguely remembered this. It was that one night when he had been invited to dinner at the Hinageshi house.

"I'm not a workaholic, and I'm not a social butterfly—but you made me feel like maybe I don't have to be! That's how I found the strength to go back to school! You changed my life, Wasabi!"

"I did...?" He hadn't even put that much thought into what he said; at the time, he had simply spoken his mind. "So I *do* have the power to help people...?"

He balled his hands into fists. *Not strong enough, my ass.*

"Thank you, Youko-chan! I'm gonna keep trying!" he exclaimed, triumphantly raising his fists into the air.

For the briefest of moments, he thought he saw her smile sweetly—but he must have been seeing things, because a split-second later, she was scowling again.

"Anyway, I gotta get to work. You sit there and enjoy your coffee. Just bring all my stuff back to the café when you're done with it."

"Huh?" Her mood swing was so sudden, Wasabi didn't know how to react.

Then Youko spun on her heel. "And for your information, that was the moment I fell for you! And now I'm madly in love with you!" she shouted at the top of her lungs. She turned and started running—then turned back a second time. "I'm rooting for you, birdbrain!"

With that, she finally dashed off, her face beet-red.

Youko-chan...is in love with me...? Stunned, Wasabi turned back to his coffee and drank it in silence, staring into space. For some reason, it tasted a lot sweeter than he remembered...

The next day, Hinako attended her very first day of Life-guard Club.

"First, you want to get someone else's attention. Have them call 119 and bring you an AED."

They were on the beach right off campus, practicing CPR drills.

"From there, your first step is to check for signs of conscious-ness by talking to the victim. Can you hear me, sir?"

As a certified lifeguard, the club captain served as the instructor for this training. He patted the shoulder of the CPR dummy lying on its back on the sand and called out to it several more times.

"No response. Next, you want to check for breathing. And if they're not breathing, it's time for chest compressions."

He placed both of his hands on the dummy's chest and pressed down firmly in small thrusts.

"One, two, three, four, five, six, seven, eight, nine, ten... You want to put both your hands on top of each other and lean your full weight into it when you press down. For an adult, you want to go about two inches deep and wait until the chest rises back up before pressing down again... Twenty-nine, thirty."

The other club members were taking notes or recording the lecture on their smartphones, but for Hinako, it was enough of a struggle just watching him do it.

"Then you tilt the head up, pinch the nose, and check for airway obstruction."

The captain blew into the dummy's mouth.

"Blow for one second, like this. Then again. While you do this, be sure to watch for the chest to rise. After that, it's time to go back to chest compressions. Five, six, seven... You want to do this for a total of thirty times."

Apparently the formal term was "near-drowning victim." Minato had received this exact same CPR twice in his life. The first time it had been successful, but the second time...

"Now then, let's have everyone give it a try...starting with Mukaimizu-san."

Out of nowhere, Hinako was summoned by name. Truth be told, she didn't want to have to do it if she could get away with it. But if she couldn't even take this first step, then she'd never be a lifeguard.

Focusing her eyes only on the dummy's torso, she placed her hands on top of each other and pressed down hard.

"One, two, three, four, five, six..."

"Uhh, looks like you're pressing a little too hard there—"

"Seven, eight—"

"THE VICTIM'S RIBS HAVE FRACTURED," the dummy's mechanical voice announced.

"You want to make sure you're only pressing down two inches and no further. Next, let's try mouth-to-mouth resuscitation."

"What?!" Hinako gasped.

But it was too late to back down. Willing herself not to avert her eyes, she slowly leaned in close to the dummy, who was wearing a face shield.

The next thing she knew, its face had transformed into Minato's.

Shrieking, she jerked back and leapt to her feet. She had never directly observed Minato's corpse, and yet the image of him cold and lifeless was vivid in her mind.

"Mukaimizu-san?"

I can't do this... I can't do this!

"Mukaimizu-san!"

Hinako ran from the beach as fast as her legs could carry her.

Hinako ran all the way to the campus pond. Gasping for breath, she peered down at the water. Her reflection was grim.

Minato... I miss Minato... Minato, help me...

She hadn't summoned him even once since the car crash...but she really wanted to see him...

"I see you—*ugh!*"

Clutching her hair with both hands, Hinako shook her head furiously. In a moment of weakness, she had nearly started to sing.

"STOP!" she screamed at herself.

The next thing she knew, she was on her way to Siren. She desperately wanted to see Youko. Surely Youko could stop her from being such a weak, wimpy coward, right? Maybe a little tetrodotoxin would make her stronger.

"Hi there!"

As she walked in, she found the blue-ringed octopus—er, Youko—bent down with her head in the dumbwaiter.

"Youko-chan?"

"Shhhh!"

Was she...eavesdropping on the customers seated on the second floor...?

Just then, a crowd of about ten young adults filed noisily down the stairs.

"And that's where we'll shoot 'em out."

"Oh gosh, that sounds fun! I've never done this before!"

"It's gonna be hella loud, so don't freak. Seriously, you'll go deaf."

"Eeee, I can't wait!"

Hinako didn't want to be judgmental, but the group looked like a bunch of stereotypical club-hoppers, from the guy with shaggy hair and a goatee, to the *gyaru* girls wearing yukatas and thick makeup, to the guys with full sleeves of tattoos. They left the café, taking their ceaseless chatter with them.

"Hey, boss! I'm leaving early today!" Youko called, pulling her apron off and setting it on the counter with her empty tray. Then she took off.

"Youko-chan?!" Confused, Hinako ran after her.

"Remember the fire that broke out at that one construction site?" Youko asked as she used her phone's front-facing camera to discreetly look behind her. She and Hinako were sitting at the front of the bus while the club-hoppers were seated at the back.

"Yeah, of course. I was living right there at the apartment complex next door."

"What? You were?" Youko looked at her in surprise. Then her eyes narrowed. "Well, apparently these people were behind it."

"What?!"

"And now they're talking about doing it again. At the abandoned OST building."

"The place with the world's biggest Christmas tree?"

The Ocean Shopping Town, or OST for short, was a twenty-story convention center that had closed down many years ago. Youko explained what she'd overheard through the dumbwaiter: In light of their failure last time around, this time the kids had brought a licensed pyrotechnician to help them shoot fireworks from the top of the building, like a Yanshuei festival. During their previous attempt, their ringleader had been arrested, but the goatee guy had gotten away.

"It's all thanks to my *brilliant escape* that we get to try again this year," he boasted to his buddies, "so I'd appreciate a little recognition. Bow to me, losers!"

"It's no use... Wasabi's not picking up," Youko sighed, staring up at the roof of the bus as she lowered her phone to her lap. "They're literally planning a crime. They're going to trespass again!"

It was now just past 7:00 p.m. The group of club-hoppers walked around to the back of the building and climbed in through a gap in the chain-link fence. Judging from the graffiti, it was clear they weren't the first people to trespass here.

"Youko-chan, this is bad news. We gotta call the cops!"

Hinako and Youko watched from the shadows as the goatee guy led the group up the stairs, leaving one person behind as a lookout.

"I'm gonna call 110!"

"We need proof! I'm gonna take photos." Youko jumped out from their hiding place and offered a friendly greeting to the lookout, as if she were one of them. Then she walked straight up the stairs.

Reeling from Youko's reckless bravery, Hinako bowed to the lookout and followed after her. "Youko-chan!"

Inside, the abandoned building smelled of dust and decay. Hinako crept along on her tiptoes.

"Youko-chan! *Youko-chan!*"

At the center of the cylindrical building was a large open area that stretched up fifteen floors, where the giant Christmas tree sat rotting.

"Wow, it's huge... Too bad it's all dried up."

Looking up from the base of the tree, it seemed to stretch on endlessly.

Crap, this is no time to get distracted!

Naturally, the elevators and escalators were all out of service. Youko immediately headed up the staircase.

"Youko-chan, wait!"

"Shhhh!"

Partway up the building, they encountered the remains of an athletic club.

"Oh, there's a pool."

Hinako followed Youko's gaze to a pool stretcher lying near the entrance. At first glance, it looked like a super-thin surfboard.

As they climbed the stairs higher and higher, they began to make out gleeful voices from the trespassers' group:

"Whoa!"

"Gorgeous view!"

"Party time, everybody!"

The sun had now fully set, and with no other tall buildings in the way, they had a panoramic view of the city lights below.

"The city's always prettiest around this time of night."

"Wow! We're so high up!"

The group was gathered out on the fifteenth-floor terrace. Once Hinako and Youko had caught up to them, they climbed onto the wall surrounding the colonnade area and concealed themselves once more. Fortunately, the trespassers were having too much fun to notice.

Just then, the goatee guy spread his arms wide and jumped from the edge of the terrace. The women screamed and looked over the edge...to find him standing on some sort of ledge.

"Oh my *God*, you scared us!"

"Let's shoot 'em off from here!"

"Okay then, let's all go down!"

Each of the guys grabbed a yukata girl and jumped down to the ledge.

"All right, now everybody grab some fireworks and let's get started!"

The goatee guy grabbed a firework shell from inside a large wooden box and held it up for the others to see. Meanwhile, the pyrotechnician ran around, inserting a red-hot metal chain into the mortar tubes to get everything set up.

Youko held up her smartphone and adjusted her position, attempting to record them. "Ugh, I can't get their faces! It's too dark!"

"You don't need to. You already have enough proof!" Hinako pleaded.

"No, I have to wait until they start firing!" Youko insisted stubbornly, crouching down on the spot.

"Ugh, fine..." Hinako couldn't exactly let Youko do this on her own, so she crouched down as well.

As they waited, a giant firework blossomed in the distant night sky.

"Whoa..."

"Looks like they're also setting them off over in Katsuura."

Come to think of it, the city of Katsuura was holding a fireworks show tonight as well. For a moment, the girls lost themselves in the rainbow-hued splendor—that is, until an ear-splitting explosion brought them back to their senses.

"Crap!"

The trespassers had started setting off fireworks of their own. Youko hastily held up her phone. Each explosion provoked squeals and cheers from the group.

"Wooooo!"

"Yeah, baby!"

The trespassers loaded the mortar tubes with firework shells and shot them off, one after another. Just then, a firework shot out from the upper terrace too. One of the men was getting cocky, wielding three mortar tubes tied together and shooting shells in quick succession, like a cannon.

"One more—boom! And another—boom!"

"Ack!" The sparks rained down on his buddies below.

"Here you go—*boom!*"

But the man slipped up, and the shell flew in the wrong direction, ricocheting off the ceiling, floor, and pillars...right toward the colonnade wall where Hinako and Youko were hiding. Both of them screamed and ducked on reflex. The shell grazed Youko's leg as it flew past and then hit the dead tree in the center of the building. Of course, nothing was more flammable than an old, dead tree. It lit up bright red, as if reliving its youth as a Christmas spectacle.

"Holy crap! Put it out, quick!" shouted one of the men on the terrace, but the man with the cannon was hyped up beyond rational thought, and he continued to shoot off fireworks.

"Aw hell!"

"Huh? What's wrong?"

"What's going on?"

At last, the group on the ledge noticed the increasingly dire problem. They began to scream and panic.

"Fire! There's a fire!"

"Let's get out of here!"

If they stayed any longer, they'd be forced to jump. Instead, they all scrambled to the ladder.

"Don't you people know better than to shoot fireworks in an empty building?!" Youko raged at them, hands on her hips.

"Can't hear you, sorry!"

"Don't know, don't care!"

And so they all ran off, with no thought given to the fire or even their friends.

"Gah!" Suddenly, Youko's leg gave out. Evidently it had been badly injured by the shell that grazed it.

"Youko-chan, we need to make our way down!" Hinako cried. The fire licked its way across the floor toward them. "The way we came is blocked now. We have to jump!"

There was no time to hesitate. Carrying Youko in her arms, Hinako leapt down onto the terrace.

"Ggghh…! That really freakin' hurt!"

Hinako had attempted to reduce the impact on landing, but evidently Youko's injury was more serious than she'd anticipated. She looked over at the stairs, where thick smoke was pouring out from below.

What do I do now, Minato? I remember you said to try to get to low ground, but…it looks like this is the end of the line!

Wasabi was on his laptop, working on paperwork. But when he went to check the date on his phone, he let out a confused "Huh?!"

His screen was *plastered* with notifications from Youko—multiple emails sent one after another as recently as one minute ago. But the most recent was a missed call notification from *seconds* ago. What was going on? Conscious of his colleagues' prying eyes, he surreptitiously checked his emails.

—Help me!

—I'm trapped in the OST building!

—Hinako's with me!

"What?!"

Just then, the wall speaker started beeping. "Outbreak in Nagakawa City, Nishikubo district 3, block 20, building 9."

That was the same address as the OST building! In a blink, Wasabi donned his firefighting gear and ran out to the pumper.

"The closest hydrant got moved 100 feet south to accommodate the new apartment complex!" he reported to Yamashiro, the driver.

"You're sure of that?"

"Yes, sir!"

After the fire at Hinako's place, Wasabi had spent his days off patrolling around abandoned buildings, including the OST.

"The girl I love is in danger!"

"I beg your pardon?"

The fire trucks all set out at once, blaring and honking in response to the fire call. The gravity of the situation was starting to sink in, and the squad captain looked angrier than ever before.

"Our ladders can't get close enough. If the fire reaches the dead tree inside, the whole place will burn like a damn incinerator!"

Sure enough, once they arrived, they found a pillar of fire flourishing in the open air, stoked by the wind.

"Found it! Thank God no one's parked here!"

Yamashiro parked the pumper in an alley near the hydrant. They'd have to climb a set of stone stairs to reach the building. Meanwhile, the abandoned firework shells continued to shoot into the night sky unattended.

"Fireworks *again*?!" the squad captain spat. "Take the hose and climb up as high as you can! The elevators are out of commission!"

"Yes, sir!"

Then someone called out code 252: trapped civilians.

"They're on the fifteenth floor! Check the other floors as you go!"

"Yes, sir!"

Once the hose was connected to the water source, the firefighters carried it up the stairs. The front of the building was packed with fire trucks and ambulances.

"Those iron doors are locked tight! Use a rescue saw and cut your way in!"

How had the culprits wormed their way into this building? One of the firefighters made a triangular cut with the saw, then reached through and unlocked the door from the other side. Meanwhile, Wasabi and his squad captain ran around to the back of the building.

"We've got traces of a break-in on the east side. We can get in through there!" the squad captain reported.

Inside, the central area of the building was a column of pure flame.

"Is anyone in here?! Say something! Anyone?!" Wasabi called, but there was no response. Together with his squad captain, he ran up to each floor, calling for survivors...but soon they hit a dead end.

"We've reached the thirteenth floor, but we can't proceed due to firework sparks! I repeat: unable to proceed! Over!" the squad captain shouted into his lapel radio...but the fireworks were so loud, it was unclear whether HQ could even hear him. "Damn it... Masks on!"

The captain reached down and grabbed the mask dangling around his neck. Likewise, Wasabi donned his mask, pointed the hose, and...

"Captain, I'm not getting any water out of this thing!"

"What?! I'll go have a look! You wait here!"

Clapping Wasabi on the shoulder, the squad captain took off back down the stairs.

Meanwhile, the rest of the team was hard at work on the lower floors.

"Current status of our informant is unknown! The fireworks have spread the fire to the stairs between the fourteenth and fifteenth floors. No 252s observed on other floors! We're told there were more than ten trespassers present when the fire broke out. Investigation ongoing!" the lieutenant reported over the radio.

Wasabi was waiting on standby on the thirteenth floor when water shot out of his nozzle unexpectedly.

"Whoa!"

The momentum was so powerful, it whipped the hose right out of his hands and slammed him in the face. Clutching his nose, he fell backwards onto his rear.

Whatever had been blocking the stream previously, it was gone now.

Wasabi lowered his hand to find the hose flailing like a raging dragon, facing off against the flame pillar without any backup. But for as temperamental as this dragon could be, it was his trusted partner.

"Rrrrgh!" Wasabi leapt onto the flailing hose, and after wrestling on the floor with it, he finally regained control of the dragon's muzzle. Together, they rose up. "RAAAAAAAAAAHHHH!!!"

Aiming the hose, he blasted away at the encroaching blaze.

Out on the terrace, Hinako leaned against the pillar farthest from the fire and rubbed Youko's back as she buried her face in Hinako's lap.

"It's going to be okay. I called the fire department, and they're right outside," said Hinako. "They're going to save us."

Just then, a massive firework exploded in their ears. Youko flinched and let out a little shriek. For as strong-willed as she could be, she was still just seventeen years old, hiding her weakness behind a tough-girl persona.

Truth be told, even Hinako wasn't sure if they would make it out of this one. The lower floors were practically a sea of flames, and it was starting to spread to the terrace.

What about Minato?

He might be able to put out the fire, but it would surely use up the last of his energy to do so...meaning he would never come back.

His words echoed in Hinako's ear: *Give me a call whenever you need me.*

No! I can't! Squeezing her eyes shut, Hinako shook her head. *If I summon him now, I'll never see him again!*

Just then, Youko started to tremble. "Oniichan...!"

She was crying. She had tried her hardest not to cry—not even during the funeral—all out of consideration for her parents, not to mention the memory of her beloved older brother. But now, at her weakest point, Youko begged for his help.

Closing her eyes, Hinako remembered what Wasabi had told her: *If you keep acting like this, he'll never be able to pass on.*

Yeah, you're right. This is what Minato would want. With a deep breath, Hinako looked up at the scarlet-tinged night sky. *Please, Minato, save us.*

"I see you there, looking at the water... Glittering sapphire as far as the eye can see."

As she sang, she could hear Minato's voice from somewhere: "Hinako... Thanks for calling me."

"Minato!"

"When my wish was granted, I was given the chance to stay with you for a little longer. Now it's time for you to grant my other wish and..."

Smiling, Hinako finished for him: "Ride my own wave."

On each and every floor, firefighters battled the blaze...until the moment a mysterious phenomenon occurred.

"Whoa!"

"What's happening?!"

A large mass of water traveled up the building, exuding clouds of steam as it extinguished the pillar of fire. It engulfed the firefighters, flushed them outside the building, and carried them up with it.

When it arrived at Wasabi's floor, he watched in awe as the giant burning tree fizzled out. Then the steam faded away, and Minato's playful grin appeared in the water.

"Looks like you're a real pro now."

Senpai?! Wasabi could see Minato, clear as day. *So Hinako-san wasn't delusional after all!*

"I'm proud to see how far you've come. Don't worry about the two upstairs—I'll rescue them." Tossing up shakas with both hands, Minato floated up and away.

Senpai!

A rush of water flooded Wasabi's feet, and he was swiftly engulfed in the torrent. As it rose, he swam down to the bottom, popped his feet out, and landed on his butt on dry land once again. The other firefighters had gone through the same training he had, so it was likely they had escaped the water the same way.

"The fire is under control. A large mass of water is ascending the building and dousing the tree," the commander reported into his lapel radio as he gazed up at the steaming building from the street below. "Source unknown."

When the water reached the fifteenth-floor terrace, Youko straightened up in alarm.

"Youko-chan, we're going into the water for a bit," said Hinako. "But don't worry—your brother will be with us."

The two girls took a deep breath...and a moment later, the water engulfed them.

"Are you hanging in there, little blue-ringed octopus?" asked Minato.

Youko took one look at her brother's ghost, and her almond-shaped eyes widened.

Oniichan! She tried to speak, but only bubbles left her lips. Grimacing, she clasped a hand to her throat.

"Say hi to Mom and Dad for me."

Say hi to them yourself, you jerk! After all the water Youko had inhaled, she was on the verge of suffocating.

Minato turned to Hinako and gestured upwards. There, several pool stretchers floated on the water's surface; he had borrowed them from the athletic club on his way up here. Hinako nodded firmly. *Got it.*

With Youko in her arms, Hinako swam up to the surface, where they gasped for breath. The ceiling was mere inches above their heads.

"Youko-chan, climb on!"

Hinako pulled Youko onto the stretcher using the same technique she'd learned in the Lifeguard Club. With Youko on her stomach, Hinako climbed on top of her and started paddling for the stairs.

"Right! Left! Right! Left!"

As soon as they made it to the stairwell, the water flooded the room as it continued to rise. They weren't going to make it.

"We're going back into the water! Hold your breath!"

But when they submerged, Minato was waiting for them.

"Once this water reaches the top of the building, it'll crash back down like a wave...and you're going to ride it," he explained as they rose up along the extinguished tree. "We're almost outside now. Youko, hold on tight!"

The mass of water reached the roof of the building and rushed outwards, like the eruption of a volcano.

"Almost time!"

The current was moving faster and faster. They shot past Minato.

"Three, two, one...!"

Then the pool stretcher flew off into the open air. Youko screamed.

"Hinako! Paddle, paddle, paddle!" Minato called from the water.

"Here I go!" With a hard look in her eyes, Hinako steeled herself for the roller coaster of a lifetime.

"Now get on your feet and ride your wave!"

Time for the takeoff! Hinako passed through tube after tube, nailing each turn at breakneck speed. As she glided down the water, she reached into the tube wall so she could hold Minato's hand. Now they could ride this wave together.

The stretcher flew out into the air as she pulled off an aerial, and when Hinako landed back on the water, another wave engulfed them. Fortunately they made it through, but the board was moving faster than her body, and Hinako lost her balance.

Crap! I'm gonna fall off!

Right as the world threatened to turn topsy-turvy, Hinako felt Youko grab her ankle and pull it back down to the board. With her help, Hinako managed to recover.

"Thank you, Youko-chan!"

Youko smirked in response. Evidently she was starting to enjoy this night surfing excursion.

The stretcher descended farther and farther, spinning in little circles as it went. Minato smiled from the tube wall as he watched Hinako fly free.

"Thank you, Hinako." Minato reached out to her as the distance between them grew. "You're my hero."

His gentle voice disappeared beneath the waves.

As the girls slid to a stop on the ground, Wasabi ran over to them.

"Youko-chan! Thank God!"

Massive relief was written all over his face. Clearly he'd found the girl that truly mattered to him.

Hinako shifted Youko into his arms and then looked back up at the building, where a golden light shone down onto the roof from the clouds above.

I guess this is where we say goodbye, huh?

Bathed in blinding light, Minato rose into the sky, holding out twin shakas—a gesture Hinako returned in kind.

Goodbye, Minato.

And as he vanished into the light, Hinako saw him off with a smile.

Epilogue

THE GIRL I LOVE is in danger!

When Wasabi said those words to Yamashiro, it was Youko he was thinking of, not Hinako. How long had he felt that way about her? Well...he wasn't sure. It just sort of happened.

"I wish Hinako-san were here with us."

It was Christmas Eve, and Wasabi and Youko were eating dinner at a restaurant with a lovely view of the nightscape.

"She didn't want to be a third wheel, duh. Oh yeah, have you seen this?"

Youko held up her smartphone to show Wasabi a news article. The headline read: FOUR MEN ARRESTED ON SUSPICION OF ARSON AT ABANDONED BUILDING. Sure enough, it was the same men who had set off those illegal fireworks—all thanks to the video footage Youko had submitted to the police.

"Don't pull any more crazy stunts like that, okay?" Wasabi pleaded.

"I know, I know!"

We're both reckless idiots, but maybe that's what makes this relationship work, Wasabi thought to himself.

"Hey, let's give Hinako-san a call," Youko suggested after they left the restaurant.

"Good idea."

Wasabi seemed to recall Hinako saying she was making omurice tonight. Ever since she had been little, omurice had always been her favorite treat, or so she claimed. Wasabi dialed her number, and she picked up right away.

"Hey there, Hinako-san! Congrats on getting your lifeguard cert!"

"Thanks! Sorry I couldn't join you tonight."

"Oh, no worries. You know, it really seems like you're riding your own wave lately," he said.

"Yeah, I got tired of the ocean. These days I'll ride whatever I can get my hands on!" she joked.

Hinako sounded like she was in better spirits, and Wasabi was glad to hear it. Tomorrow was the anniversary of Minato's death, and they had made arrangements to visit his grave together.

"Here, I'll let you talk to Youko-chan."

"Merry Christmas, Hinako-san! Being single is for squares, you know!"

Hinako giggled, and after they wished each other a happy new year, the call ended.

"So, where to?" Wasabi asked.

"Oh, how about the Chiba Port Tower?" Youko suggested. "Hinako-san told me they have this place called the Lovers'

Sanctuary. You can write a message on a heart-shaped card or chain a heart-shaped padlock to the rail—all sorts of stuff."

As Wasabi stared back in silent surprise, Youko scowled.

"What's your problem?"

"I'm just surprised. It sounds like the sort of thing you'd call cringey."

"W-well, I figured *you* might be interested, that's all!" Blushing beet-red, Youko turned away.

Wasabi smiled and took her by the hand. Sure, Youko could be foul-mouthed and stubborn, but to him, she was adorable.

I'm glad I let them have the night to themselves.

Smiling, Hinako hung up the phone and looked up at the Chiba Port Tower. Soon they would turn on their Christmas tree illumination, and couples would flock to the tower in droves, just like last year.

At that moment, she happened to look down and notice a small puddle of water by her feet.

"I see you there, looking at the water," she sang quietly, experimentally. But the water's surface didn't even ripple.

Bit by bit, she was starting to move on. But no matter how much time passed, it still felt like icy wind was blowing through a gaping hole in her chest...especially on nights with a lot of happy memories attached to it, like this one.

But right before the sadness could overwhelm her, the music started to play, the Port Tower illuminations flickered to life... and she heard a name she wasn't expecting.

"We have a message from Hinageshi Minato-san to Mukai-mizu Hinako-san. This one was submitted to us one whole year ago!"

What? Hinako stared up blankly at the tower.

"Merry Christmas, Hinako! From now on, let's spend all our Christmases together...forever and ever and ever!"

Minato must have submitted it while she wasn't looking. He'd always loved surprises... He must've been so sure they would visit the tower again this year...

Guess what, Minato? I've gotten really good at making omurice.

"Nnn...hnnnn..."

And I've learned how to write the kanji for Hinageshi.

"Nnhnn...aah...waaaah...!" Unable to hold back, Hinako broke down sobbing.

Meanwhile, amid the glow of the Christmas lights, the first snow began to fall.

Spring had rolled around once more. But this time, Minato wasn't around to enjoy it with Hinako.

When she arrived on the beach, surfboard in hand, she greeted the young male surfers hanging out nearby.

"Hey, guys! We've got a trench in the area, so stay safe, okay?"

Trenches were deep grooves carved into the ocean floor by strong currents in shallow waters. A less-than-cautious surfer could easily get trapped and drown.

"Yes, ma'am!"

The young men watched Hinako go with looks of admiration on their faces. You see, this college-age lifeguard was something of a celebrity at Kujukuri Beach...

"I guess there's no more waves coming."

"Maybe we should call it a day."

The other surfers turned and headed back to shore...but not Hinako. She sat and waited, the wind silently ruffling her hair. All she could hear was the whoosh of the water—

Wave incoming!

"Hinako! Paddle, paddle, paddle!"

Hinako could hear Minato's voice on the ocean breeze...

"Now get on your feet and ride your wave!"

But this time, she would ride it alone.

With her eyes on the horizon, Hinako plunged forward.